Adventures of Siberian Cat Katerina

Adventures of Siberian Cat Katerina

Book One

Leonid Prymak

Writers Club Press
San Jose New York Lincoln Shanghai

Adventures of Siberian Cat Katerina
Book One

Writers Club Press
an imprint of iUniverse, Inc.

For information address:
iUniverse, Inc.
5220 S. 16th St., Suite 200
Lincoln, NE 68512
www.iuniverse.com

Any resemblance to actual people and events is purely coincidental.
This is a work of fiction.

ISBN: 0-595-22497-0

Printed in the United States of America

Dedicated to my
sweet daughter, Irene

Contents

Foreword

The first time I told this story, it was to a sweet girl named Irene, who happens to be my daughter. At that time she was eleven years old going on sixteen. Now, she is a very successful lawyer in New York City. She still loves my story, *The Adventures of Siberian Cat Katerina.* This is why I have decided to share this story with all intelligent and adventurous children. It is a story about an unusual and talented cat, and this book is the first of many. She plays tympani in the symphony orchestra, has a beautiful singing voice, and in one of her benefit concerts sings selections from the musical *Cats.* Also, Katerina is the only known cat who successfully completed medical school and became a founder of the International Medical Center for Pets. The reason she decided to do this is because she speaks all the languages of the animals of the day and creatures of the night. When the Medical Center for Pets has a patient that a doctor cannot communicate with, Katerina comes to the rescue and tells the doctor exactly where it hurts, helping the doctor make the proper diagnosis. As busy as she is with her singing and concert performances with the symphony orchestra around the world, she always finds time for her friends at the International Medical Center for Pets. I hope Katerina will win your heart as she won the heart of my wonderful daughter, Irene. And now, it's time to turn the page and enter the challenging world of Katerina the Siberian Cat and her best friend, Irene.

My best wishes to you on your journey.

Your friend always,
Leonid Prymak

Part 1

Adventure of the flying spirits

It just happened to be that this story began in the beautiful Virginia countryside, on a small and very lovely Christmas tree farm called "Evening Star", where there lived an eleven, going on sixteen, year old girl named Irene.

Her father, Peter, many years ago came to wonderful America from Russia and decided to settle in Richmond, Virginia. He was a talented violin player with the Richmond Symphony Orchestra. Since musicians in the Richmond Symphony Orchestra, as in many other orchestras in America, didn't make a lot of money, Peter had to find another way to support his family. It was a very big project for him to do on his own and he needed a lot of help. He borrowed money from his old friends and the bank and bought a little farm where he decided to grow Christmas trees for grown ups, all small and not so small children to enjoy. The best part of being a Christmas tree grower was that Peter didn't have to water the trees because they grew to be beautiful by themselves. This gave him a lot more time to play his violin. To play violin in the symphony orchestra is not an easy job and one must practice, practice and practice.

Irene's mother, Maria, was an elementary school teacher and a very lovely lady. She taught first grade and loved her job and all of her students very much. Since she also loved to garden, helping Peter with the Christmas tree farm was a joy for her.

At the age of eleven, Irene was a rather accomplished musician. She played piano since she was six, won a few local piano competitions and already had public performances of her own with pretty nice fees for each concert. Half of the fees she saved for college, but the other half of her fees she insisted on giving to her father to make payments for the Christmas tree farm and make his life a little bit easier. He did put up a small fight about accepting the money from his daughter, but in the end, he was very happy to receive her gift. In gratitude, he bought her a grand piano that he was able to restore to its previous grandeur. A good grand piano cost a lot of money in our days.

Irene adored her magnificent grand piano and practiced a lot. She shared a lot of beautiful and sometimes very frustrating moments with her piano when she had to start working on new and very hard pieces of music. At a very early age, Irene learned that playing well is not an easy job. Sitting at the piano or any other instrument and practicing for hours at a time can be very lonely, especially when you see all your friends doing their normal stuff like playing video games and watching a lot of TV. But, Irene loved to play so she didn't really mind not spending more time with her friends.

It was spring, and in the springtime it became a tradition for many musicians from the symphony orchestra to come with their children to Peter's pot luck plant your tree party. Indeed, it was a very unusual party filled with laughter, music and planting their own Christmas trees. For his guests it was easy work because the ground had already been plowed up in preparation for planting the new trees. The trees on the farm were all different ages and the field they used for the planting party was always the one where all the trees had been cut and taken home by Peter's customers for the Christmas just passed.

Donald, Carol and their daughter Ariana were the first ones to arrive. Ariana was a very good violinist. She played in the Richmond Symphony Youth Orchestra and brought her violin with her. Irene and she were long time friends and liked to play music together. Peter saw them as they parked their car and came out to greet them.

"Donald! Carol! *Kak dela?* (How are you?)," shouted Peter, giving them both a big hug. "Hello, Ariana. Are you going to play violin for me today?" asked Peter and took her violin case.

"Yes, I will, and I brought some music with me so that Irene can accompany me."

"Great, we can have a little musical treat for everybody," commented Irene.

Peter guided them toward the house. "You should come visit us more often, not just when it is fir planting time. You know the door is always open for you," said Peter.

"You know our schedule, Peter. Carol has to ride her horse Zantas and Ariana has to ride her horse and we always play concerts or rehearse on weekends and then there is school during the week. Whew, it makes me breathless just to say it! It is so hard to find the perfect time to visit you. Now at least we combine pleasure and helping you with planting your new Christmas tree crop," answered Donald who was a drummer in the symphony orchestra. His wife, Carol, played violin and for many years was sitting in the orchestra with Peter on the same violin stand. As they were walking into the house another good friend of Peter's, bassoon player Lynda and her son David pulled next to the first guest car. Peter waved to both of them and yelled. "Hi, Lynda, I'm glad you brought your son David with you. We need strong muscles around here. Please make yourselves at home. My place is your place. Just walk into the house."

In a very short time, Peter and Maria's house was filled with musicians and their children. Musicians were chatting about the orchestra, who was leaving the orchestra to go to play in another orchestra, and who got the job and was coming into the orchestra as a new member.

A large, jolly man walked into the room. On his head he was wearing a crown and was holding the hand of a little girl with a crown on her head and a recorder in her hand. "King Michael and Princess Jordan. We came to join you in your musical celebration of your new fir planting season," announced Michael. He played English horn and was one of the funniest people in the orchestra. During the Christmas season, when the orchestra was performing *Nutcracker* with the Richmond Ballet, whenever the Arabian dance was danced on the stage, Michael would put on his Arabian mask. This mask had an enormous nose and a big mustache and looked very funny. Michael saw the smiles on musicians faces but would play his instrument like it was nothing unusual, cracking up most of the musicians and making them laugh in the orchestra pit. He was also a great candy maker and, as always, brought to Peter's party a big box of his special candies.

"Children first and grown ups later," he said putting the box on the table.

"Mmm, Mikey. They are my favorites. I hope there will be some left for me," said Peter.

"If you get lucky," said Irene and opened the box. She walked around the room and the children each picked one. They were wonderful milk chocolate candies, which were made in the shape of little Christmas trees. After all the kids had their pick, she came to her father and nodded to him to take one.

"I'm so lucky to have a daughter like Irene," said Peter and popped the chocolate in his mouth. "Mmm mmm, it tastes so good, Mikey. You should open a candy shop. You'll make ten times more money selling candy then playing in the orchestra," said Peter. "Speaking of playing, are we going to hear our young stars anytime soon?" Peter turned to Mike's little daughter, Jordan. She brought her recorder to her mouth and started to play a simple song.

"Yes, yes, let's play some Mozart." Encouraging her, Peter went to bring Ariana's violin. In a second his room was filled with the most beautiful and richest arrangement of Twinkle, Twinkle Little Star ever heard. The children were competing with each other on their musical instruments trying to out play each other. Irene sat at the piano and started to play the melody in very sophisticated chords. After a few virtuoso passages they ended the song and big applause filled the room. By now, every one was stuffed with food, candies and drinks.

"Now it is time to make donuts. Whoever wants to help me plant the magic trees, please follow me," said Peter and a crowd of musicians and their children followed him to the tract of land where they were going to plant their trees.

"Who has the honor of planting the first tree?" asked Peter.

"The smallest kid on the block," said Lynda, and pointed her finger at Jordan, who played recorder so wonderfully. Her father, Mike, reached for the tree and gave it to her. Young Christmas trees looked like skinny sticks, about a foot long with bare roots. All Jordan had to do to plant it was make a small hole with a garden trowel, stick it in the hole and then gently press the dirt around it. The whole process took less than a minute. In a few hard working hours, old and young musicians' hands planted an entire strip of land with the new Christmas trees. The sun was coming down and the pile of Christmas trees disappeared rather quickly into the ground. The party was over and everybody felt a little bit tired but very happy.

~ ~ ~

When a young person decides to become a good piano player and good musician, time becomes scarce and has to be wisely divided between piano practice, school, homework, reading and playing with friends. But music and playing piano was Irene's first love and real passion. Music would take Irene to a different world that she could create with her music. Also, she knew that later in life, no matter if she was going to become a big concert pianist or not, music was going to add great fun to her life. It would let her see things in many different colors, colors that people who do not play instruments may have a hard time seeing and understanding.

There is nothing more gratifying then being able to express yourself through music and musical instruments. Just touch the keys of the piano and magic suddenly appears in the air. Music can say and express what words never can. This is why so many songs are written and loved and sung by people. The words can be great but if you take the melody away from them, they die.

Music and the arts were very important parts of Irene's parents' life and so they became in hers. Irene's mother and father enjoyed her beautiful piano playing and were very gratified to have a daughter like her. They loved their daughter and would do almost anything to please her, because she was a pleasant, caring and sensitive child who rarely whined. She was an excellent student in school, very good in math, but her most important achievement was that she mastered the Russian language because she had a grandmother, Rose, who didn't speak English. Irene wanted very much to communicate with her Grandmother Rose, without the help of her father, and to do so she had to learn Russian. Irene loved listening to her grandmother tell stories about her father when he was a little boy.

It was a weekend and after practicing her piano for an hour, Irene saw her father Peter walk in to the music room.

"Hi, Irene. How is your practice going?" asked her father.

"I'm doing fine but some music that I decided to play is very difficult," she replied.

"What is so difficult?" asked Peter.

"I've been asked to play for our school assembly and decided to play something that all kids in school will want to hear and can relate to," replied Irene.

"Let me guess what it could be. *Star Wars* by John Williams? I've heard you working on that music."

"Yes, I've been trying to learn it in the last two weeks but it is very hard."

"Well, let me see the music," said Peter and joined Irene on the piano bench. He took the music from the music stand and glanced through the 44 pages of the book.

"Wow, Irene. This is very difficult stuff you are trying to play. Let's see what we have here. *Main Title, Princess Leia's Theme, Cantina Band. The Battle, The Throne Room and End Title* It is a lot of music, Irene, and this arrangement by Tony Esposito, whoever he is, is very hard. He must have written it for himself. Are you sure you would be able to play it all?" he asked and looked at Irene with a big question in his eyes.

"I don't know, Dad. I would like to, but I don't have that much time to learn it. There is just not enough time in the day for everything I need to do."

"Don't worry, Irene. Let's take this music apart and see what we can do to make it easier for you." Peter opened the music of *Star Wars* and started to slowly read through it. Irene was patiently waiting until her father went through all the music and was ready to give her advice on how to approach her music project for her school.

"Okay, Irene. I think I know what you should do to make it possible and not break your neck trying to learn everything in this music. First, you don't have to play it all. In the orchestra when we play *Star Wars* music, some times we make cuts from the musical score. You can do the same. Just choose the movements that kids in your school would be most excited to hear. Second, it is just for your information, but if you miss a few notes no one would ever notice it. I have played this music many times in the orchestra and I have to tell you, some of those passages are so hard and go so fast that it is almost impossible for us professional musicians to play it all. Most violinists in some of the places just zoom through those passages and don't play all the notes, but it sounds like they did. If we try to play all the notes, we may get stuck like a truck in the mud and slow down. Since the musical score is like a clock, we have to be on time to meet the other instruments. No one would wait for them if they would slow down to get through all of their notes. This is an old orchestra trick of the professional musicians. Be on time is the most important thing and if it is possible to play all the notes it's great and if not, no one is going to send us to jail for missing a few notes. Understood?" Irene laughed and nodded yes.

"See, Irene, you just learned another way, another secret language of the professional fiddler. Don't tell it to anyone, okay?"

"Yes, Dad. I promise I'll keep your secret with me."

"You are already doing well, Irene. Do you know that you know three languages now?" said Peter and proudly smiled at his daughter.

"Three languages?" asked Irene, and Peter nodded yes. "I thought I speak only two languages, English and Russian. What is the third one?" she asked her father.

"You don't know what is your third language, Irene?" She looked at her father and shook her head no. "Music, Irene. Music is your third language and it is a very special language that doesn't require any alphabet, only musical notation. Did you think of that?"

"No, I never thought of that the way you do, Dad," she replied.

Her father continued. "Just think, Irene, music is a totally different language. Look at all these notations," said Peter and pointed at the music. "If you show these notations to some one who doesn't read music, how do you think it would look to them?" asked Peter.

Irene thought for a second and replied with an intelligent answer. "I think, Dad, it would look to most people like a foreign language."

"That is right, Irene. It would look like Russian for people who live outside of Russia and never read anything in Russian. Music has its own language with very special notation; it is sort of like a different alphabet, Irene. You probably don't know that. Important aspects of different languages are that quite a few of them use different alphabets. Now stop and think for a moment. What would the Russian alphabet look like to people who read and speak English?"

"It would look very strange. It did look very strange to me when I saw it for the first time," replied Irene.

"Right again, Irene. The English alphabet looked very strange to me when I saw it for the first time, Irene. This is why the Russian alphabet would look strange for some one who knows only Latin / English or English /Latin alphabet." Peter paused for a moment, looked into Irene's eyes and continued. "Russian is very hard but it also is a very poetic language, Irene. It happens that it uses not Latin, but the Cyrillic alphabet which was invented by Saint Cyril in the 9th century. As you can see, we are just at the very beginning of our civilization. So many Russian writers are very well respected and are known all over the world. They have to be grateful that Russian was at their disposal as a great set of colorful paints, brushes and beautiful country site for the famous artists. Now you have your answer concerning what the Russian alphabet and Russian is all about. You can share it with your friends at school. I'm sure not all of them know what you just have learned now," said Peter. Irene nodded yes and Peter continued. "How many countries do you think are using this Russian or Cyrillic alphabet?" he asked and Irene shrugged her shoulders.

"It is a very hard question for me to answer, Dad. I'm not an expert in this area," said Irene.

"Let me see if I have the right answer for you, my dear daughter. I can't guarantee to you that it will be the perfect answer, after all I'm only a musician and not a linguist," said Peter and saw Irene frown. "Is it the word linguist that you didn't understand, Irene?" asked Peter.

"Yes."

"A linguist is a specialist in different languages. I knew one many years ago, a fellow who spoke eleven languages. He was a real linguist. I don't think there are many people like that on this planet, Irene. Well, since now you know what a linguist is, let's see if I can come pretty close to finding countries which use the Cyrillic alphabet, Irene. Let's try to count those countries together," said Peter and looked at Irene.

"First country is Russia, then we have Ukraine, Belarus, Bulgaria, Serbia, Slovenia and maybe a few more small ethnic regions in the Yugoslavian Republic like Montenegro and some others. What other countries that you know of may use a totally different alphabet from the Roman alphabet that is used in English and other languages? Let's count them and see if we are right. Arabic language countries and there is a bunch of them and we are not going to count them one by one. Then what do we have, Japanese, Chinese, Georgian, Armenian, Korean, and the ancient Jewish language of Hebrew," said Peter, who thought for a moment and continued. "May I ask you, Irene, why did you learn Russian?" asked Peter. Irene looked at him with the look of surprise in her eyes and was just about to answer her father's question when he interrupted her.

"I think I know why, Irene. I think you did it for some one you love very, very much. You did it because you wanted to communicate with your Grandmother Rose on your own, without your father's help of doing any translating for you. You wanted to have a heart to heart conversation with your Grandmother Rose, right?" asked Peter. Irene nodded yes and Peter continued. "When I brought my parents from Russia to America, your Grandmother Rose didn't speak any English. Do you know why?"

"No."

"The reason why, Irene, is because she came to America from Russia very late in her life. She and my father found a community of other Russian speaking people here in Richmond so she never had to learn English. Now, what can you tell me about what you have learned from your Grandmother Rose when you spoke Russian with her?" asked Peter.

Irene thought for a moment and replied. "I've learned many things, Dad. I've learned that Grandma was a respectable, retired oral surgeon in Russia and many times decorated veteran of World War II. I also remember and would never forget that Grandmother Rose was the one who taught me how to walk and how to talk. The first words I've ever said were in Russian. Sometimes Grandmother Rose would tell me about her days as a field doctor in the hospital in the Russian army during World War II where America and Russia were partners and fought their common enemy together. She had to do a lot of hard and challenging work as a doctor. She told me that on some occasions during the war, she had to pull wounded soldiers from the front line and be very innovative performing all kind of surgeries even though she was only trained as an oral surgeon by the School of Dentistry. I was surprised to learn about Grandma, because when you look at her physically she is a very small and fragile woman but also I think she is a very strong individual. When I think of what she did, I think that she is made out of steel. Also, I remember that she would tell me a lot of stories when I was a very little girl. Some of the stories she told me were about you and your beautiful Siberian Cat Vassya and how much fun the two of you had together. He was a very unusual cat and like you, Dad, he liked pickles very much, and pickled tomatoes. I wish I could see your cat Vassya's face when he was eating pickles," said Irene and laughed.

Peter smiled and replied. "Oh I remember my cat Vassya, Irene. I remember him very well, like I was just with him yesterday. When I would eat pickles he would look in my mouth and scream very loud asking me to share them with him. Vassya was very unusual for a cat to have this kind of taste and like things that mostly humans would normally like. At the time when my cat Vassya lived, there was no cat food in Russian stores. It is not like here in America where you see aisles of food for pets. When I first came to America it shocked me when I saw it with my own eyes. At that time I thought that there is more food for pets in America then food for people in Russia." Peter paused for a few seconds and continued. "You know, Irene, Vassya is a very common name for the male cat in Russia and I bet the country of Russia was probably populated with at least a million Vassyas!"

As Peter said that, one of the funniest of her grandmother's stories popped into Irene's head. It was the story her grandmother told her many times when they were alone, the story about her son, Irene's father, when he was just a young boy and loved to read a lot of adventures and scary stories. One time he got his hands on a book by the very well known American writer Edgar Allen Poe. One night, Peter read a few of Poe's stories and got very scared. Really, really scared as little boys can get when they read in their bed very spooky stories late in the evening before they go to sleep. Peter got scared to the point that it was absolutely impossible for him to fall asleep alone in his own bed. He could not close his eyes for a moment and his pride wouldn't let him admit that to his parents.

It was very late in the evening and Peter was begging his cat Vassya to stay in bed with him and to be his protector and make him feel safe from his spooky thoughts. In the beginning, his cat Vassya agreed but then like most cats, he changed his mind and started slowly his escape to freedom, gently crawling from under the blanket. Irene thought that being a Siberian Cat, Vassya probably was feeling very hot from being under the warm blanket in Peter's bed because of his lush and very thick fur and Peter's body temperature. Combined together it made it impossible to keep Vassya's promise to Peter to stay in bed with him and play a protector for that horrible night. Irene knew that as a little boy, her father didn't know that. As Vassya was trying to get out of the bed, Peter was pushing and pushing with his hand to get the cat back under the blanket. The patience of Vassya came to an end and he got very mad at Peter. He probably screamed some bad cat words that could not be translated to Russian or any language. Vassya took a fearless bite on Peter's little nose, screamed and with the roar of a winner jumped out of the bed and ran like a mad cat out to the kitchen to have some cold water and cool himself off. This was the very first time in Peter's short life that he had his first out of body experience and traveled to the far away galaxy of stars. He didn't follow his cat Vassya and his scary thoughts flew away into space like a rocket. Even now, many years later, Peter still had some small traces from Vassya's bite on his nose. It looked as his cat Vassya left his mark on

Peter's nose as if he wanted his master never ever to forget him and his beastly behavior on that memorable and scary night.

"I'm thinking of your first out of body experience, Dad," said Irene and looked at her father. "Do you still remember it?" Irene smiled at her dad. She was just about to burst out laughing but tried very hard to contain herself.

"Gosh, do I remember it, Irene? You better believe it. I remember every moment of that late scary evening." Peter shook his head. "I remember it, Irene, as it just happened to me last night. Things like that I would never, ever forget," said Peter, embracing Irene. "I don't know how many kids would like to learn more about out of body experiences in general. I guess an out of body experience can be induced by many different things. Sometimes people may have this happen to them when they are in very dangerous situations or near death. I had a few out of body experiences, Irene. Vassya's bite on my nose brought me to my first out of body experience, but there were a few after that," said Peter and looked at Irene.

"Can you tell me about your other ones?" asked Irene. Peter looked at his daughter, put his hand on her head and made a little mess of her hair.

"I don't know, Irene, if you are old enough for me to tell you things like that. It is somewhat outrageous."

"Please. Dad, tell me. I really would like to hear it from you."

"Well, okay. I guess we can have a small chat, father to daughter, about my past experiences, Irene. Let me think, where do I start? Okay, here it goes, Irene. When I was a little boy, I had repeated dreams that one day I was going to come to America. Not only did I have these dreams, but on a few occasions I had visited Richmond, Virginia in my dreams."

"You did, Dad?"

"Yes, I did, believe it or not, Irene. Later in life when I first came to Richmond to audition for the Richmond Symphony Orchestra, I stayed in a hotel in downtown. I had a little bit of time on my hands and walked to Capitol Square. When I came close and walked through the gates I recognized the Capitol building and surrounding landscape. I had seen it in my dreams before or was it that I have seen it in my out of body travels?" Irene looked at her father and he read some skepticism on her face.

"It is very hard to believe that one can visit places so far away, Dad," said Irene.

"Yes, I know, my sweet Irene, that it is outrageous, but it is the truth, Irene. Of all people, you are the one I don't have to make up any story about those things. I'm sure I'm not alone. Who knows, maybe somewhere on this planet another girl is asking her father how is it possible to happen? I just hope that some parents would be more open-minded and explain to their children what it is or get them a book where they can read about it. It is a very hot topic in our days, Irene. Past lives, out of body experiences and reincarnations. Books on all of these subjects, including alien abductions, often become bestsellers. Actually, some of them are rather interesting and were made into pretty good movies. I know for sure, Irene, that some kids sometimes ask their parents about all those things. I hope that their parents would not laugh at them and can give them an intelligent answer or at least help them to find some books and have the time to explain to them this rare phenomenon of our time," said Peter.

The story about the nose bite of cat Vassya made Irene laugh very hard. Some times she would come close to her father so that he would not suspect what Irene was up to and look at his nose trying to see traces of Vassya's sharp teeth. Many times she asked her father to tell his version of that story but he never did. He probably was too embarrassed that his mother Rose told it to Irene. It was the first time he opened up to his daughter as they were sitting together on the piano bench and Irene wished it could happen more often. She loved to hear stories from her father; he was filled with them. But, dear readers, sometimes there are stories in our dark closets that we wish no one would know except us and that was one of those stories. This story about the nose bite must have brought feelings of pain and itch on Peter's nose. It is why he probably tried to stay away from telling it to Irene. Instead, he told her another story about his cat Vassya. This story was not funny at all but, rather, a scary one with a happy ending.

"Are you ready for another story about my flying cat Vassya?" asked Peter and Irene nodded yes to her father. Peter thought for a moment trying to compose his thoughts and began his story.

"One day, Vassya and I played a rather popular game among kids of hide and seek. In Russia it was as popular as it is here in America. It looks as if children like to play the same games all over the world and it doesn't make any difference what country they live in. I remember it as if it happened to me yesterday. It was summer time in Russia and, as I recall, Irene, it was a very beautiful and warm day. Your Grandma Rose opened all of the windows in our apartment to get some fresh air. We lived on the fifth floor of a big building. I think that building had over two hundred apartments. We lived in apartment number forty. You probably don't know it, Irene, but most people in Russia live in very big apartment buildings, not like here in America where a lot of people live in their own houses. I don't know if any violinist in Russia is a Christmas tree farmer like I am. But anyway, let me get back to my Vassya story. When I was a young boy, my beautiful cat Vassya and I loved to play our favorite game of hide and seek. When I would hide and he would find me he would attack me fiercely, like he wanted to make sure that he was the real victor and won the game. My cat Vassya didn't like to lose. We chased each other for some time and both got tired from running and playing the game. I took a little nap and when I woke up the first thing I did was call my cat Vassya. I waited and waited but didn't hear Vassya's answer. He must have seen me taking a nap and I thought he would respond to me right away because he always was a very big talker. I tried again and again hoping that

Vassya would finally say hi to me in his friendly cat meow. But there was silence. So, Irene, I got very scared. I looked for him everywhere and thought that Vassya found a great hiding place or possibly disappeared from our apartment through the open front door. I asked my mom if she saw Vassya anywhere or maybe he skipped outside for a walk. She shook her head no and I began to seriously worry about my cat Vassya. After I looked all over the apartment I came to the open window and looked down. Five floors below, on the ground next to the building, I saw my best friend, my beloved cat Vassya sitting near the bush, scared and very quiet. I quickly ran down the stairs and found him laying down and trying to hide from people's eyes. I gently asked Vassya if he had any broken bones or if he was all right. Vassya didn't move and looked at me with a very scared look in his eyes. Gently, I picked him up and brought him home. Fortunately for me, Irene, Vassya was not hurt. He flew down five floors and landed on his feet thus saving his own life. It was simply amazing. When Vassya was a little kitten and I was a very bad boy, I threw Vassya up into the air many times just for fun. As I did I noticed that Vassya landed on his feet again and again every time. I gave Vassya good landing lessons. He mastered landing on his feet and it must have saved him later and added to his life another cat life. You see, Irene, you may never know when you may have to use the knowledge you acquire in the past. The more you know, the better it is. The more you know, the better prepared you are to enter your life. You master the piano now, then later you can always give piano lessons. Experience counts for a lot. There is nothing like life experience, Irene. Trust me. It helped me a lot in my own life."

Irene was listening to her father and he read on her face that she was very fascinated with those stories about his cat Vassya. But little did he know, more than anything in the world, Irene wanted to have a Siberian cat, one who could be her very special friend. The cat she could play with, talk to and cuddle. As you know, children and grownups sometimes have bad dreams. Those dreams are very real and at the time of your dream you cannot tell if it is a dream or it is really happening to you. This is the scary part of the bad dream. There is nothing better at that moment than having a special pet with you in bed. You feel very secure and if you open your eyes your cat is there for you to cuddle and hold close to yourself when you are scared. Often at night, Irene would drift off to sleep and dream of her special pet, a Siberian cat. It had to be a cat. Why? Cats really can sleep for a very long time and also cats could be very playful when they are awake. It is fun just to watch them play, even if they only play with a simple piece of paper. Irene knew that for her, it had to be a Siberian cat because of her father and grandmother's funny stories about those big, furry Siberian cats who, if they would have lived in this country, would be definitely mistaken for dogs because of their very large size.

As they were sitting together on the piano bench, Peter thought of how Irene was extremely fond of her grandmother Rose and would go to visit her as often as she could. At the same time, Irene thought of the stories she heard from her grandmother. Stories about how rich was Russian soil on raising in its unfortunate land great writers, composers, dancers and the most incredible performers on every single known instrument. She told her that most world class chess players and champions also came from sad Mother Russia. But despite all of those things, she heard from her grandmother another type of story. Often her Grandmother would let her know how happy she was that her son and Irene's father, Peter, was living in a great place like America. She told Irene about how grateful she was to her new land for accepting and embracing her in her old age. She often reminded Irene that there is a lot to be proud of to be an American and be born in this wonderful land of freedom.

Irene hugged her father and asked, "Could I have a Siberian cat as you did when you were a boy?"

Peter thought for a moment and replied. "You know, Irene, how much I love you?"

"Yes, I do, Dad," she answered.

"I'd like to promise you a Siberian cat. If it would be possible to locate one in America, I'll get it for you, Irene. I do have a very close friend in the New York Philharmonic orchestra, he is also from Russia and a musician. He plays viola in the orchestra. I think he has a young, and very beautiful, Siberian lady cat named Ludmilla. Let me call my friend Sergei later this evening and ask him if he would try to find you a kitten," said Peter and thought that it might be very hard to find a Siberian kitten for Irene because there were only a very few Siberian cats in America. (Cats from Russia could not travel freely at that time like cats from other countries.)

~ ~ ~

In a conversation later that evening with his friend, Sergei, Peter found that Sergei knew a very famous Russian ballet dancer. This amazing dancer, Rudolf, lived in New York City and had defected to America while on a concert tour with the Russian *Bolshoi Theater,* or Grand Theater if one wanted to be exact and translate the name into English. It was the first defection from Russia and it created a lot of publicity and all kinds of diplomatic noise. Russia was humiliated and very embarrassed by his defection, but could do nothing about it. He broke through the iron curtain and was free to live in the New World. That famous Russian ballet dancer had very carefully planned his escape from Russia to America with his Siberian cat, whose name also happened to be Vassya. He escaped from Russia because he didn't want to be the property of his government and was looking for his artistic freedom as well as his human rights. Not all countries could say that they have those freedoms and rights. He had chosen America and New York to become his home.

The next day Sergei telephoned this famous ballet dancer and in two weeks, after a few unsuccessful attempts, was finally be able to reach him at his home. Not many people know that big stars in ballet, opera and very good piano, cello and violin players travel a lot from one city to another, from one country to another and hardly spend any time at their home. It is rather glamorous but also a very difficult life to live. When Sergei finally reached his friend he asked him if his cat Ludmilla and Vassya could get married and have a baby kitten for the talented girl Irene, from Virginia. Like most Russian ballet dancers, Rudolf had a very warm, giving soul and passionate heart and agreed for his cat, Vassya, and Sergei's cat, Ludmilla, to be married.

In the true old Russian tradition, the bride and groom received a wedding herring, which being cats, made them very, very happy. Soon after their marriage, Vassya and Ludmilla had a beautiful baby girl Siberian kitten. Irene's father Peter received a phone call from New York City with this wonderful news. Irene could hardly wait until her kitten grew big enough so that she could take her home to Virginia.

In the month of December, Irene and her father went to New York City to visit Sergei and his other friends in the orchestra, and to get the Siberian kitten, which Irene named Katerina. You may ask a question, why did Irene name her cat Katerina? Well, for many reasons. First, because Katerina was a Siberian cat and Irene thought that a Russian name was just perfect for the Siberian cat. Second, her Grandmother Rose. She thought her grandma would be very pleased to hold in her hands a Siberian cat with a Russian name that would remind her of her young age and her homeland. A person's roots always remain. It does not matter where the person came from to America, either a happy and prosperous country, or an unhappy and poor one, the fondness for the homeland persists.

Katerina had a very fluffy, soft coat of fur the rich color of red gold, and big blue eyes that were unusual for a cat. They were so deep and sensitive that anyone could fall in love with Katerina instantly, which is exactly what happened to Irene and every one in her family. The first time Irene picked up Katerina in her hands, Katerina gave her a kiss with her rough little cat tongue. Irene gently stroked her under her chin and Katerina rewarded her by purring and curling into her lap, falling fast asleep. Irene was holding her in her arms and did not wish to disturb her beautiful kitten. Sergei and Peter saw that perfect picture and didn't want to disturb them. Peter looked at his friend Sergei and at the same time they both softly whispered to Irene that she should stay with Katerina until she would wake up from her kitty nap.

Irene gently carried Katerina to the sofa and lay down with her, putting carefully this charming little fur bagel on her chest. It was so great to lay down together with this amazing little kitten. Irene felt very happy, with Katerina's warmth penetrating her chest. They both looked happy and slowly dozed off. As Irene departed into her sleep together with Katerina, she had an interesting dream. It was a vision of her and Katerina flying high in the air to many strange and exotic places. Dream worlds can be very fascinating for people of all ages. Not only do people dream but pets can dream, too. If you have a pet and would observe your friend very carefully when your pet is asleep, you will notice how they dream and see visions. Cats may smile and actually laugh; dogs softly woof and their paws quiver as if they are running. People can see in their dreams things from the past and maybe what may happen to them in their future. What pets see in their dreams is hard to tell because they don't tell the contents of their dreams to humans, whereas we always share our dreams with the people who are close to us. Sometimes our dreams can be so incredibly beautiful that we wish they would become a part of our real life. Sometimes our dreams can be so bad that we wish we had never, ever seen them at all.

Irene's grandmother Rose, as her father Peter, had some very unusual abilities. They both had a strong psychic ability and could see in their dreams events from the future. Irene came from the same line and also inherited this rare ability but she didn't know it yet. When Irene opened her eyes, she saw that Katerina was already awake and squirming on her chest. When Katerina saw that

Irene was awake, she stood up and stretched her little body in that way that only cats can do, arching her flexible body like an archer. She yawned and Irene saw her small, sharp, perfectly white baby teeth. Their eyes met, and Irene knew she had a very special gift from her father, the best gift she could ever wish for.

Katerina, as fate would have it, was born from a line of very artistic and noble Siberian cats, a line of cats that were very artistic and familiar with ballet and music. Cats can be gifted like people. There are no two cats alike. It was clear to Irene from the moment she brought Katerina home to their small house on the farm. She practiced piano a lot and her father, Peter, had to practice violin. Katerina was absolutely hypnotized by the sound of Peter's violin. It was not that she didn't like the sound of the piano, but the voice of the violin was what she could listen to for hours. It is well known that the sound of the violin is the closest instrument to the human voice and that is probably what won her tiny heart.

Whenever Peter would get ready to practice in his room and tune up his violin, as soon as she heard the sound of his violin Katerina would run to his door. When the door was closed, Katerina would gently scratch the door with her paws until Peter would let her in. He remembered himself that as a boy when he was practicing his violin, his cat Vassya would do exactly the same things. He could listen and watch Peter play his violin for hours. Watching Katerina would bring to Peter a lot of his childhood memories and not necessarily all good ones. His nose was itching on many occasions when Katerina was watching him play his violin. As soon as she would enter the room, Katerina would jump on the big, poofy chair in the corner of the room, turn around once or twice in a circle until she found just the right spot to lie on. Peter always waited until Katerina got comfortable in her chair. He would put his violin under his chin and gently stroke the strings with his bow, letting Katerina know that he and his violin had become one. He slowly would start with his warming up exercises and build up the speed until his fingers felt comfortable on the violin fingerboard. In a short time they would be flying all over the fingerboard as if they were running away from bad dreams. From where Katerina was sitting, it looked like a long stair and Peter's fingers would be running up and down the stairs as notes on the violin went from the very low to the very high as the fingers would climb the stairs.

Musicians usually call those stairs exercises playing scales and they can play them for a long time because they are very good for fingers and help them in developing good technique and perfect intonation. You may ask what intonation is and who works on intonation? Any musician who plays any instrument except piano works on intonation. On the piano, we have keys, and all of the strings are tuned by the piano tuner for the piano player. This is why a violinist and oboe player sometimes would envy a pianist, because the pianist doesn't have to work on perfecting intonation. If the piano is out of tune, there is nothing the pianist can do about it but blame the piano. String players, violinist or a bass player for example, would have to blame only themselves for playing wrong notes. To play the violin or any other string instrument, musicians have to tune their own instrument all the time or when it gets out of tune. Weather can affect tuning a lot. In the wintertime, violins can go out of tune like they are mad at the cold weather, as if they have aches and pains. In the summer, they are more agreeable, enjoying the warm weather like we all do. But Peter can explain it better.

Irene, too, liked to listen to her father practice. She was not surprised to find Katerina lying in the chair. Irene did not disturb her and found her own comfortable spot in the room, curling up on the sofa. Her father finished playing his scales and once again found his violin out of tune. He turned to Irene and remarked, "I can't wait for the warm weather to come. It is so hard for my violin to stay in tune in December. Do you know the reason, Irene?" asked Peter.

Irene thought for a moment and replied, "Is it because of the cold temperature?"

"Yes, Irene. It is because of the cold temperature outside. Changing from the cold temperature outside to the warm temperature inside makes all the difference. Sometimes our tuning pegs pop out like corks from a champagne bottle," explained Peter.

"Something else is different on the violin then any other instruments, am I right, Dad?" asked Irene.

"Yes, Irene. On the violin there is no set place or dividing lines on the fingerboard for the violin player's fingers to land. It is a guessing game and the violinist must know his violin very well to put his fingers on the right place at all times. It only becomes precise after lots of training. You are actually training the brain and muscles to work together."

"Do violin players miss their notes sometimes?" asked Irene.

"Oh boy, yes, they do. Sometimes it happens in concerts and it is very embarrassing. This is why practice makes them better. For the violinist, playing those exercises like scales doesn't sound like great music, but we all have to do it to keep our hands in good sporty shape. All musicians must warm up their hands before they start playing very hard pieces of music otherwise they can strain their muscles and develop all kinds of aches and pains which later in life may become fatal to their musicians' profession. There are well known cases when talented musicians stopped playing their instruments because of those misfortunes. French horn, tuba or trumpet players have to carefully watch their lips and strings and piano players must be very gentle with their hands. Just like sportsmen may have sport injuries, musicians can have their own injuries related to their own instrument. Playing violin is one of the most unnatural things to do. Just holding a violin is rather difficult and very uncomfortable. It is not like sitting at the piano where all keys are looking at you and inviting you to touch them. If you sit down on the keyboard of the piano with your little tush, the piano can still make a pleasant quality piano sound. I would not advise you to sit on the violin or cello. All you would hear is a big boom-boom, as the instrument broke under the weight of your body. If you try to do it you are asking for big, big troubles. You probably don't know this, but violins and cellos come in many different sizes."

"Why?" asked Irene.

"Why? If you are a small kid and would like to start taking violin or cello lessons, you cannot play a full size cello or violin."

"Why?" asked Irene again.

"Why? Because the hands and fingers of children are too small, this is why you can find a mini-violin for a three or five year old young musician. If you have the right size of violin or cello, you can reach the notes with your small fingers perfectly. Now please tell me, Irene, about playing the piano," Peter requested.

Irene thought for a second and responded. "Piano is very different from violin and cello. Piano is the same size for any age and little kids have to wait until their hands and fingers grow big enough to reach an octave on the piano. I remember very well how I had to struggle when I was little and it was very hard for me to reach an octave with my small hand. An octave is a distance from one C to the next higher C. So, the distance between two different C's or any other notes like D—D, G—G would equal an octave. It is very hard to stretch an octave for a small kid," said Irene and Peter continued, developing Irene's thoughts.

"You are right, Irene. Some pianists are known to have very large hands and they can reach far beyond an octave. Just to compare, for a moment, a pianist with a basketball player. Most basketball players can hold the ball easily with one hand. For the pianist with large hands with long fingers, playing octaves on the piano is just a like eating a piece of cheese or chocolate cake. I think, Irene, we covered it all about our instruments," said Peter, finalizing their discussion.

When Peter practiced, he liked to watch how Katerina would not miss any of his movements, her head nodding up and down in sync with his bow so that she looked like she was saying 'yes'. Peter loved to play great melodies for his own enjoyment. Two of Peter's favorite pieces of music were Mendelssohn's second movement from his violin concerto because of its sweetness, and a beautiful violin solo from the movie *Young Frankenstein* because of its passion and crazy content in relationship to the character in a scene in the movie. You should see that movie and I guarantee you, the violin melody will win your heart like it won Katerina's.

Sometimes he played this melody just to remember how it goes. Human memory cannot last forever without it being refreshed. On some occasions, Peter had to refresh his strolling violin music and would play a lot of familiar tunes from the musicals and movies just to keep them in his fingers. Peter was very well known in Richmond as a strolling violinist and could entertain people at different parties for hours with just his violin and his funny stories. His story about his cat Vassya and his first out of body experience was one of the most popular.

Whenever Katerina heard the melody from *Young Frankenstein,* she would close her eyes and purr the melody in unison with the violin like she was ready to fall in love. It was rather unusual to hear the melody purred by a very young cat. As Peter was looking at Katerina listening to his violin playing, he often thought of his childhood cat Vassya and his strange taste for food. I guess Siberian cats were somewhat different from other known cats. Not only did they look different in their appearance, but also no one could ever predict what was on their independent minds and what they would decide to do next.

~ ~ ~

Irene never had a sister and always wanted to have one but unfortunately her mother, Maria, couldn't have any more children of her own and adoption was the only option. On the night before Christmas, Irene made a wish before she went to bed. She asked for her dear cat Katerina to become her playmate like a little sister, so they could tell each other their most intimate thoughts and share their biggest secrets. Believe it or not, this is what happened on that special and very strange night in the country in Goochland County in the beautiful state of Virginia.

As the warm winter blanket of the night softly tucked Irene in her bed, and as the moonlight gently caressed her hands, she fell deeper and deeper into her sleep. When she was fast asleep, she began to dream. A vision of her and her parents decorating their Christmas tree appeared right in front of her. This vision just came out of nowhere like a Polaroid picture. Irene saw as her Siberian cat, Katerina, was very curiously circling around the Christmas tree. Katerina sniffed and touched with her soft paw all of the Christmas tree ornaments as if she was trying to inspect them and make sure that they were worthy of her first Christmas tree.

After the tree was fully dressed in its Christmas decorations, it stood glowing and beautiful, as beautiful as a young lady ready for her first debutante party. It is still a live tradition in Virginia and for some families in Virginia, debutante parties were still popular. Irene's father, Peter, played his violin at a few of them in Richmond and nearby counties. Irene stood back and admired her Christmas tree as if it was a most exquisite work of art. What made it even more beautiful and exciting was that the tree came from Irene's own Christmas tree farm, "Evening Star".

That tree had the most fascinating scent, a scent that in one second would take you into the special kingdom of a magical Christmas tree forest that just grew around the corner from her house and within the reach of her hands.

The angel at the top of the tree seemed to come alive and signaled for the lights on the Christmas tree to begin their dance. Brilliant patterns of rainbow colors sparkled throughout the tree. In those colors Irene recognized a beautiful dance from *The Nutcracker*, a ballet that she saw for the first time when she was just four years old. Over the years it grew on her and she was able to play on the piano music from some of the scenes from the ballet.

Peter always played that ballet with the Richmond Ballet and almost always took Irene to the dress rehearsals of *The Nutcracker.* She only missed it once when she was sick. On one occasion, Peter introduced her to the magnificent pair of Russian dancers, Igor and Marina, who were dancing the star roles in the ballet. It was fun for her to speak to them in Russian and she still remembered how graceful and elegant they were. Now they were dancing in one of the best ballet theaters in Europe and she truly missed seeing them on the stage. She heard from her father that when they won silver medals in an internationally known ballet competition, they were immediately invited to join a ballet company by another well-known European ballet.

Irene's vision continued and at the end of the dance, the lights twinkled for the final chord, letting her know that the piece of music was over. Irene could not believe what she was seeing and stood as if frozen under a magical spell. All of a sudden, a mysterious force gently lifted her from the floor and slowly carried her to the top of the tree. Irene was floating in the air like a bubble in a champagne glass. She felt totally weightless. When Irene came closer to the little angel at the top of the tree, she noticed the angel was smiling at her. A soft blue light shown from the angel's eyes.

"My dear, young lady," whispered the angel. "You made a special wish before you went to bed and because you are so sweet, giving, honest, and warm-hearted, your wish is going to be granted. Look down now."

Irene looked down and saw her friend Katerina the Siberian cat standing on her back feet and waving with her right paw, calling "It's me, it's me, Katerina the Siberian cat. Please take me with you!"

Confused, surprised and happy, Irene looked in the eyes of the angel with great joy. The angel smiled and winked. When Irene looked down at Katerina again, she saw her dear friend slowly floating to the top of the tree. As Katerina reached her, Irene saw the angel flap its wings and fly to them, extending her hands to Irene and Katerina.

"You are my dear guests for this magic night," said the angel. "I am going to take you on a journey that will always live in your memories. And now, please do not be afraid of your weightlessness or the fast speed of our journey. We are going to visit some other different countries of the world, where we can see how different cultures celebrate Christmas. We will see a few different Christmas trees. I hope you guessed by now, I am not just an ordinary angel, I am an inspector general for Christmas trees. Once a year, I fly around the world to see the best decorated Christmas trees and leave surprise gifts for special children. You and your friend Siberian cat Katerina are to be my helpers for the judging contest of the Christmas trees. Hold onto my hands. Here we go!"

~ ~ ~

Together they flew through the walls of Irene's house, high into the clear sky. They were not bothered by the cold air and didn't feel the high speed of flying because they became special flying spirits.

"Where are we going, or should I say flying?" asked Katerina.

"First," replied the angel, "we are going to the country of Brazil. We are going to visit a little boy by the name of Heitor Villa-Lobos. He is very poor and made all of his Christmas tree's decorations by himself."

Irene interrupted. "How do you know which country to visit and whose house to go to?"

"I know everything there is to know about Christmas trees," answered the angel. "And I go to see the Christmas trees in the countries and houses where only the most sincere, kind, big-hearted and generous children live, the ones I can be proud of." The angel looked at Irene and Katerina as they all were flying with very high speed. Their hands tightly held the angel's hands and it made them feel very special.

Minutes later, they landed in one of the poorest villages in Brazil. They entered a very small house that had only two rooms. Three young children lay asleep in one of the rooms. The angel pointed to the little boy who had made all of the Christmas decorations for the tree. "It took him a long time to make them. For some, he used paper and others he carved from wood," whispered the angel. The most interesting ornament was a tiny carved horse and wagon. You could see every hair in the horse's mane and tail, as if he put his very soul into the carving. "It took him a year to make this," said the angel. "He has a very special gift." The angel moved closer to the tree and admired the carved ornament for a moment longer. Smiling, she looked at Irene and Katerina and touched the horse with her finger. Immediately, the ornament turned into pure gold the color of Katerina's fur.

"Why did you turn it into gold?" Irene asked the angel.

With a mysterious look in her eyes, the angel answered, "Heitor prayed for money to help his younger brother, who is very weak from a heart condition he was born with. He needs an operation to stay alive and the family does not have the money to pay for it. The gold ornament will be more than enough to pay for the operation." They took a final glance and were soon high up in the sky, speeding their way to another destination.

"How wonderful it is that there are real angels who can listen to the voices of children and come to help them," Irene said. The angel looked at Irene and smiled.

"Where are we flying now?" asked Katerina.

"Katerina and her questions. You are a true cat filled with curiosity. We are making a stop in the middle of the ocean in the country of Iceland," said the angel. "Iceland is a small country surrounded by a very cold sea. The land of Iceland is filled with volcanoes and geysers, which Icelandic people use to heat their cities."

"What are geysers?" asked Katerina.

"The volcanoes are very hot. They heat the underground water and turn it into steam. Sometimes the steam escapes and makes giant water fountains shoot into the sky. That's a geyser. In America, you have a very famous geyser, Old Faithful." The angel continued. "The roads in Iceland are extremely icy in the wintertime. Iceland holds the world's record for people falling and breaking their bones. It is not unusual to see many people on the streets of Iceland's cities walking with crutches. But it is still a beautiful and very peaceful country."

The angel, Irene and Katerina flew over the capital city of Reykjavik. They were invisible as they soared through the brightly lit streets of that beautiful Nordic city. They stopped at a neatly painted house on a cobbled street. "A little girl named Christa lives here," said the angel. "She loves to play the violin. It is your favorite instrument, Katerina, right?" Katerina nodded yes and the angel continued. "Christa was working on a piece of music by the Norwegian composer Edvard Grieg, and wanted to play it as a surprise for her grandmother. But she fell on an icy road in her beloved country and hurt her little pinky on the left hand. As you know, on the left hand you have to use all your fingers to play violin. If it would have been her right hand pinky she could probably manage to play her song. Accidents do happen and Christa was not able to play for her grandmother. She was crying a lot and very upset over what happened, but there was nothing she could do. It's going to take weeks for her pinky to heal."

"Oh, that's terrible! Poor Christa! I don't know what I would do if I hurt my fingers and could not play my piano. I truly understand her feelings. My heart is going out to her I feel so sorry to hear about her injury. How can we help her?" exclaimed Irene.

"Well, my dear Irene. That's why all of us are here," the angel replied, "Christa made a wish before she went to bed, just like you did, Irene. She asked for her finger to heal fast so that she could play the violin for her grandmother and make her feel very happy."

"Oh, I love the sound of the violin! I can listen to it endlessly," said Katerina.

Irene asked the angel, "Do you know my father plays the violin in the Richmond Symphony Orchestra?"

"Yes, of course, I know everything about you and your family, Irene."

Katerina interrupted. "It is my dream to play the violin but look at me, I don't have any fingers, not even a pinky," said Katerina and held up her paws.

"This is not a big problem, Katerina. You can play a lot of different musical instruments that are used in the symphony orchestra and still become a great musician," said the angel, "Just look at the kettledrums or as they call them in the symphony orchestra 'tympani'. I can see you will become a great tympani player and a wonderful musician, and you won't need the kettledrum mallets. I guarantee you will excel at more than one instrument."

Katerina became excited. "Are you saying that I'm going to have more than one talent?"

The angel looked at Katerina, smiled and nodded yes. "I could name a few, Katerina," said the angel, "but you will have to be patient, my dear Katerina, and wait for events to unfold." The angel waggled her index finger at Katerina. "All in good time, Katerina. All in good time."

They flew through the window of Christa's house. Christa was still in bed, soundly sleeping. Her left arm lay across her stomach on top of the quilt and they could see the small splint around her pinky. The angel touched the splint and it vanished. Irene saw Christa stir and move her fingers in her sleep, as if she was playing the violin again. Before leaving the house, the angel, Irene and Katerina circled around the Christmas tree, turning on the tree's lights. In the lights the Christmas tree stood up in the house like the creation of a talented artist and Irene and Katerina could see how beautifully it was decorated. From looking at the tree anyone could see how much love Christa and her family put into decorating their Christmas tree. It was filled with traditional Icelandic decorations.

"Now we are about to take our longest trip, so please hold on tight to my hands," the angel said to Irene and Katerina.

"Where, where are we flying now?" asked Irene and Katerina together.

"We are flying to the largest country in the world, a country that is filled with hardship and sadness. It is a country where so many beautiful and great things have been created over the entire history of that nation. Where do you think it could be, Irene?" asked the angel.

"Hm, could it possibly be Russia?" asked Irene and the angel nodded yes and continued.

"Not only are we flying over the entire country of Russia, Irene, we are flying to the coldest part of Russia where Katerina's roots come from. Now I have a question for Katerina. Where do you think that could be, Katerina?"

"Well, since my parents are Siberian cats, it must be my never seen ancestral motherland Siberia, am I right?" asked Katerina.

"Yes, Katerina. Your answer is brilliant. It is the land of your ancestors but it is not your motherland," replied the angel.

"Oh I understand it now. I am a Siberian cat but because I was born in America it makes me an American, right?" asked Katerina.

"Right, Katerina. I also know your parents, cat Vassya and cat Ludmilla. They are truly wonderful Russian cats but you are a Russian American cat."

"You know my parents?" asked Katerina, surprised.

"Yes, I do. Your father, cat Vassya, was in great danger when his master, Rudolf, one of the greatest ballet dancers, decided to take him out of Russia to America. But he was very brave and very quiet in Rudolf's suitcase. Not many cats can exhibit such bravery, Katerina. You should be very proud of your father."

Katerina's eyes got very wide and she replied, "Wow, I never knew that about my Papa. He was very brave, but I'm so glad that he and his master Rudolf defected and I have been born in America."

Katerina proudly looked at Irene and Irene chimed in, "I'm glad I was born in America, too. My father did the same thing. He masterminded his exodus from Russia. He and my grandparents were born in Russia," she paused, looked at Katerina for a second and sighed. "Is that why I always saw a Siberian cat in my dreams?"

The angel glanced at both of them. "Special magical forces brought you and Katerina together, Irene. The two of you have a great future ahead. You'll make great contributions to mankind."

They flew very high into the air so that Irene and Katerina could see more of the giant country of Russia. They were so high that Irene felt like they could touch the stars. The land of Russia was completely covered with snow and looked like the world's largest snow blanket, with many black spots of different sizes scattered along it. These small black spots were the villages and bigger ones were small towns and cities. It was a breathtaking sight. There was open space in front of their eyes as far as they could see from their wondering heights. The angel read their thoughts and elaborated on them.

"Russia is a very big and mysterious country that in its deep past was very religious," explained the angel. "Now it is a country where it is considered a big crime to believe in god and read the bible."

"I can't imagine a country where you cannot read whatever you want. Something like that could never happen in America," said Irene.

"You have a lot to be thankful for, Irene. America is like no other country in the world. It is a land of freedom and free spirit. I always liked to visit America but I have so much to do in less fortunate countries around the world," said the angel.

Soon they were floating in the air above a small Siberian village called Parhomovka.

"Look down, my friends. Now we reached our destination." They made a sharp dive down from the sky and hung over the little house. "This is the place where the little boy Alesha and his parents live," said the angel.

From where they were, Irene could see that it was a small, old village. Most of the houses were made out of logs and wisps of smoke were coming from the chimneys. Irene was very excited to see so many small houses with their wisps of smoke. It reminded her of a doll theater where all of the toys were on strings. All you would have to do is pull the strings and the doll would come alive and start to move.

"Before Alesha went to bed on this special night before Christmas, he made a wish. He wanted to have his own bible so that he could read it by himself and enjoy the stories. Having a bible in Russia is not as simple these days as it was many years before, when each town had a lot of churches. Christmas used to be a great celebration in Russia. Now they do not celebrate Christmas as religious holidays are forbidden," the angel said.

"Oh, how horrible!" exclaimed Irene.

"Yes, it is horrible," the angel replied, "but it is not going to be forever, Irene. New and uncertain times will be coming to Russia soon, just wait and see."

"How are you going to give Alesha his bible?" asked Katerina.

The angel smiled. She knew that she had a special bible for Alesha, a bible that would be his very own. They landed in front of Alesha's house. It looked just like all the others. They flew through the chimney, down the pipe into the kitchen stove. The oven door opened and they found themselves in a warm room. Irene and Katerina were surprised to see Alesha sleeping in a loft above the country style stove. Irene touched the stove with her hand and felt how warm it was.

"Now I know why he's sleeping up there!" Irene laughed.

"Yes," the angel said, "this is the warmest place in the house and parents give it to children to keep them very warm."

From the kitchen they flew into the big room where the Christmas tree stood.

"They have Christmas trees in Russia?" Irene asked.

"They don't call them Christmas trees anymore. The name Christmas tree was changed for their government ideology. Now it's called a New Year fir or as you would say in Russian, 'Novogodneja elka'."

"Wow, novogodneja elka," Katerina repeated it.

"Novogodneja elka," Irene slowly repeated. She looked at the angel and shook her head. "It should be called a Christmas tree," Irene insisted.

"I agree with you, Irene. And I can tell you that one day soon it will be called Christmas tree like it always was called for centuries," the angel said.

"Do they have Santa Claus in Russia?" Katerina asked.

"What do you think, Irene?" asked the angel.

"If they don't have Christmas trees, they probably don't have Santa."

"Yes, Irene. They don't have Santa anymore. They changed Santa's name also and call him Uncle Frost. He is the one who brings presents to the children in Russia." With those last words Irene and Katerina suddenly saw a box appear in the angel's hands.

"What is that?" asked Irene.

"What is inside of this box, can I see it?" added Katerina.

"This is a magic set of the game 'Scrabble'. Do you play Scrabble, Irene?" asked the angel. Irene nodded yes and the angel continued. "The letters in this magic box of Scrabble have special powers and upon Alesha's request they will rearrange themselves into words, sentences and verses from the bible. No one will ever be able to find out how Alesha could learn the stories from the bible. All of the letters in this special 'Scrabble' game are in Russian. The letters look very different from what you are used to seeing. They are in Cyrillic. Your grandmother, Rose, reads a Russian newspaper that your father Peter orders for her from New York, Irene. Have you noticed how different the letters look from the English that you are used to reading?"

"Yes, I know that. I speak some Russian but not as good as my father and Grandma Rose. I tried to read the Russian newspaper to my grandma Rose, but I read it so slow that it puts her to sleep. I guess I'm too small yet to read the newspaper," replied Irene.

"Am I also too small to read newspapers?" asked Katerina.

"I don't think cats can read newspapers, Katerina. To be able to read the newspaper, first you have to learn the alphabet and go to school. We cannot take our pets to school with us. They have to wait for us at home. This is a fact of life, Katerina," said Irene.

"It should be changed," said Katerina with a sad sigh. "I would love to go to school with you and sit at the same desk. I promise I would be a very good student. I bet if I would try hard I could make honor roll."

The angel smiled, looked at Katerina and said, "There is always home schooling, Katerina. You can always do your school home work with Irene and if anything will be too difficult for you or you would not be able to understand, you can ask Irene's mother Maria, her father Peter or Irene. Maria is a very good teacher, and she can always find the time to help Katerina, right, Irene?" Irene looked at the angel and nodded yes in agreement.

"Yes, yes. How come I didn't think of it?" Irene replied with a smile on her face.

"Because little girls can't think of everything. People don't think of everything, Irene. This is why there are so many troubled places in this world. I wish all people on Earth would stop and think for a moment and become one with beautiful nature and love and embrace everyone on their planet. Do you know that there are other planets like Earth in this universe?" asked the angel.

"Really? How do you know that?" both Irene and Katerina asked at the same time.

"I know a lot of things. I've visited many places in our universe. Earth is one of the most beautiful planets and your people should do everything possible to get along and avoid any wars and distractions or if they are not careful they may destroy the world as you know it," said the angel.

"Is it possible that our world could be destroyed?" asked Irene, and the angel silently nodded yes.

"I hear my dad and my mom talking about the news on TV and what bad shape we are in today," sadly replied Irene.

"Yes, Irene. I see it all the time from where I am," said the angel and paused for a second. Irene and Katerina held tighter to her hands and saw that they were flying over the ocean. The angel continued. "This is why you are here with me now. You and Katerina are on a very special mission. You are to become special ambassadors of our good will and help your world to become a better place for all of you to live in."

"I'm an ambassador of the angel?" Katerina's tail went wild.

"Yes, you are, Katerina," said the angel and looked at Irene with piercing eyes. There was something very unusual in those eyes. Irene had never seen eyes like that before. The music of the famous Rachmaninoff second piano concerto gently entered her thoughts. It was a total surprise for Irene. She knew that concerto very well and it was her dream to play it is well as the great pianist and composer Rachmaninoff played it more the half a century ago before his death in 1943. She was totally hypnotized by the music. The veil from her eyes was slowly disappearing and once again her eyes met with the eyes of the angel. Irene hesitated for a second and popped her question.

"Your eyes look so different from anything I've seen before in my life. Are you an angel or are you an alien angel, or an angel from another planet?" she asked.

The angel smiled and responded with a lot of warmth in her voice. "I'm all of those things, Irene. If you like, you can call me an angel or if you like you can call me an alien. As all people on planet Earth, we aliens from a far away world also have names," said her mystery host and in the background piano concerto music continued but a little bit softer.

"What is your name?' asked Irene.

"My name is Forra and I'm from the planet Tycho," said the alien.

"Forra. Ms. Forra, nice to meet you," said Irene and gave the alien her hand. She took her hand and Irene felt as Forra was very deeply connected to her through the physical contact with her.

"We are here to prevent your people from going down the path of total destruction, Irene. We know so mach about your planet. The people on your planet are on a very dangerous road. Unfortunately, we cannot do anything about it except spread our word and knowledge among Earth people. I'm sure you have heard about aliens visiting your planet in the past. Some of our visits have been described a long time ago in many legends of the people on Earth. There were many movies made about our arrival on the planet Earth but none of them were close to reality. I'd like you to know that we've been watching you for thousands of years. We have always been your friends, Irene." With Forra's last words, Irene for the first time could see herself lying on the examining table and saw friendly but very unusual faces looking at her. It felt as the curtain was totally lifted from her eyes and she was brought into real time. Music was still flowing in the room and she looked around and found herself in a room that looked like it could have been a hospital room. She began to feel scared and the sound of music became louder. She looked at Forra again and felt an alien hand on her forehead. Immediately it brought to Irene a feeling of peace and calmness in all of her body. The music was telling her that anyone who would love to listen to that music was not capable of doing any harm to a little girl. She knew that it was going to be all right. Some internal message was sent to Irene's nervous system.

"Where am I?" asked Irene.

"You are on our spaceship. It is a small craft that came here to your planet on a very short visit. We all live on the big craft that is a size of your small city," said Forra and looked into Irene's eyes.

"Is it like our space station near the Earth?" asked Irene.

"No, Irene. Your space station is as big as a lifeboat on the Titanic. Our ship is as big as the Titanic and the spacecraft you are in now is as big as the lifeboat, too. Does that help to answer your question, Irene?" Irene nodded yes. Her head was spinning and she thought of how many other things she wanted to ask the alien. Forra read her thoughts and continued her explanation. "I can see, Irene, you would like to learn so many things about our civilization but I don't think it is possible for me to tell you all in the short time that we have together. You are our very special guest and I'll do my best to answer some of your questions. Unfortunately we don't have the time for us to tell you all that you would like to know about us. We don't have enough of your Earth time as we have to meet our mother spacecraft soon in space. It would take a very long time, Irene. But we will give you the keys to learn and find out more about us. The key is in your hands," said Forra and Irene looked at her hands but didn't find any key.

"Did something extraordinary happen to me? Am I all right?" asked Irene.

"Yes, Irene. Indeed, something extraordinary happened to you," responded the alien. Irene saw a vision of her. A picture of an angel and an alien changed a few times in her head like she saw it in a kaleidoscope.

"Nothing bad happened to you, Irene. You are all right and now you are healthier then you have ever been before. You have been immunized from a lot of things. One of them is juvenile diabetes. On the planet Earth, people cannot yet be protected from many horrible diseases, and autoimmune disease is one of them. We vaccinated you and your cat Katerina from many bad things, Irene. We need you and Katerina to stay healthy for a very long time," answered Forra. Irene looked at Forra and was surprised to see her big dark beautiful eyes. They were much bigger than human eyes. The hands of the alien also looked very young, without any trace of wrinkles or aging spots on her skin.

"How about my cat, Katerina. Is she okay?" asked Irene.

"Oh, yes, your cat Katerina is fine. She is now exactly as you wanted her to be, Irene," replied Forra.

"What do you mean by saying 'she is exactly as I wanted her to be'?"

"Well, Irene. Katerina is very different now. She looks the same but she is able to talk. Didn't you want her to be your sister?" asked Forra and Irene nodded yes and thought of how in the world the alien possibly could know her wish that she made before she went to bed. Once again she was very surprised with Forra's answer.

"For you it is almost impossible to believe, Irene, but for us it is a very simple thing to do. We tapped into your memory card and read everything you ever learned and thought of in your short child's life. You did ask about your sister and you wanted Katerina to become one since your mother Maria cannot have any more children. Now you have a sister, Irene. It is your Siberian cat Katerina. She can talk and think like you do, Irene. In a very short time she will know more then you and many people on your planet, Irene," said Forra. Irene was totally overwhelmed with so much information, that even to her sounded absurd and outrageous.

"Memory card? What is that? I don't think we have memory cards." Irene remained skeptical.

"But you have a brain which stores a lot of information, Irene. We can read all the information that has been deposited in it over the years. We can even see your first reaction on coming into this world. We can trace all aspects of your development from the day you appeared on this planet. We have the knowledge and technology to do it. Yes, it is outrageous from your human point of view, Irene, but it is a part of our life and what we learned in many more years of development then mankind has."

"How is it possible for a cat to become like you and know more than many educated people? Why didn't you make me like that?" asked Irene.

"It is a very interesting question again, Irene. Like you, we experiment first on animals. We only experimented with your cat Katerina. Also we don't want to create a super human out of you or any one else, Irene, or people will think you far superior then them and make a god of you. Being something of that nature could be very dangerous in your world. If we had done that to you, Irene, it was going to change your life and make you a subject of constant study in your research institutions. We don't want that for you. Your cat Katerina is enough at this time, Irene. It is possible for us to do it with your cat Katerina because we injected her with accelerating development serum; also, a lot of what we know is deposited in her yet very small brain. One of the very important aspects of that is a scanner that will allow her to memorize pages of your books in seconds. In a very short time you will be able to see it, Irene. It is widely used on our planet for thousand of years. The serum does a lot of different things and one of them is it mutates important brain cells. Mutation changes brain development in a very short time. You on your planet are using a very small portion of your brain's potential. We have learned on our planet many thousands of years ago how to utilize all of our brain cell's potential and how to isolate any bad cells prior to birth."

"Are you super beings?" asked Irene.

"Yes we are, Irene, and your cat Katerina is a super intelligent cat now. You remember movies about Superman and Supergirl, don't you?" Irene nodded yes again.

"Why did you do that?" she asked.

"Very good question, Irene," replied Forra and touched Irene's hand. "We did it to show your Earth people how intelligent we are, what we have for our pets, and how intelligent our pets can be. Cats not only make great pets but also serve us as our perfect companions. They do not require a lot of space for exercise and are compact animals. They have a very neat appearance. Historically, cats were one of the first domesticated pet animals on both of our planets, Irene. They are great on very long space travel in the galaxies. Their vocal cords could be easily reconstructed, or as you say fine tuned, for them to communicate with you in your human way, using vocal communication," explained Forra.

"Do you have cats like ours on your space ship?" asked Irene.

"Yes, we do, Irene, and they are absolutely adorable. We brought one to show you and your cat Katerina," said Forra.

"You speak English so well. I'm sure you don't have English classes in school on your planet. Where did you learn your English?"

Forra smiled at Irene and answered. "From space, Irene. We watch your television programs like news and see what is happening in your daily life. We also can see your movies, the ones shown on your television. Two hours of your TV program we can see in just five seconds of your time. We record all of what is shown on your TV and then we see it all on our screen at a different speed. I'm one of a few on our ship who has to study Earth affairs. This is why, Irene, I'm here talking to you now," explained Forra.

"How is it possible? Do you understand all of the Earth languages?" asked Irene, and shook her head in total disbelief.

"Most of them, Irene. The proof is right here in front of you and you can touch me to make sure that I'm not a dream or an illusion. As you can see, we are at a very different stage in our development then you on your planet, Irene. Do you remember when I told you that we are using all of our brain?" asked Forra and Irene nodded yes. Forra looked at her and continued with a smile on her face. "I already told you that we can watch your programs in different speed modes, but we also can read pages of your books in one second and remember everything. We are far advanced in our development then your people are on this planet. You have some people who have photographic memory and it is considered an extraordinary gift to have on your planet. In my world it is just normal. We all have that gift. You sleep six to eight hours. We sleep two to four hours. We have twice more time to learn and create," concluded Forra.

"I'm beginning to understand it now but this is absolutely incredible and just so hard to believe," responded Irene.

"I'm glad you are beginning to absorb what you hear. I would not find that incredible as you do, Irene. Our civilization is many times older then yours and our technology is far superior to yours. If I would compare your Wright brother's airplane to your newest space agency ship, would you be able to see the difference between you and us, Irene?" asked Forra.

"Yes, we studied the Wright brother's achievements in school and I know it was the beginning of our aviation. Now we are far advanced into a new computer technology world," said Irene.

"Yes, I know. We know exactly what you studied at school, Irene. As you can see, in the last 100 years you came a long way and it is just a beginning. Just think, Irene, where your civilization will be 1000 years from now. You only discovered insulin in 1921. Before that time all people who got juvenile diabetes died, now you can save them and control this condition. You only discovered penicillin in 1929. What about human and animal organ transplants? It is very sophisticated for your doctors and your medical field. But for us it would be an ancient method. We cure things in a different way, from the inside, long before they go bad. We have vaccines for everything. In our society no one gets sick or catches a cold and our life span is way over 700 of your earthly years. We live about ten times longer then the luckiest people on Earth. Also, we learn about 100 times faster then your people. How old do you think I am?" asked Forra.

Irene thought for a second. "Is it possible that you are 200 years old?"

"Yes, Irene, it's possible except that I am twice as old as that. Would you believe me, Irene, if I tell you that I'm 597 years old and consider myself just in my prime? I'm just like your father and mother would be," answered Forra.

"How do you stay so young for so long?" asked Irene.

"It is very simple, Irene. Once a month in your Earth time, I hook up my body to my personal purification station. What it does is the total diagnosis and cleansing of all of my systems. It is almost like your car. When your car starts running poorly you take it to the auto mechanic and let him diagnose what is wrong with the car and fix it. My personal diagnostic system very thoroughly checks me on all possible things that can go wrong with me. It finds all my weak points in my engine and fixes them before they would give me any problem. It flushes out all my dead and sick sells. Pretty amazing, right, Irene?" asked Forra.

"That is amazing. Looks like you have a personal doctor or a clinic following you everywhere you go," replied Irene.

"Yes, Irene. You are absolutely right. My personal wellness station is a large clinic like your largest hospital with the greatest knowledge you can possibly imagine. But it all comes in a very small box. It is very hard to describe. I would not even try do to so. But I tell you the simplest and most important things about our life. We exchange our blood for artificial blood or as you would call synthetic blood very soon after our birth. If you'd like to know exactly, it happens within 48 hours of your earth time after we are born. At the same time we are going through our immunization process. Now you can understand why leukemia, as it is known on your planet, has been cured on our planet more then ten thousand years ago just by substituting our blood for artificial blood. You see how simple it is, Irene? What more can I add about our health care system? Our skin is very elastic and almost impossible to cut and as a result of that we almost never bleed. We never have any colds or fever as it is known on your planet."

"Now I understand how different and sophisticated you are."

"I'm glad you do, Irene. We are counting on you and Katerina to help us to make contact with your people and educate your world about us and our world," said Forra and read that Irene's thoughts shifted to her cat, Katerina.

"How different is my cat Katerina now?" asked Irene.

"She looks the same. Please come with me and see for yourself," said Forra and helped Irene get up from the examining table. As they approached the wall it opened and Irene saw another alien in a smaller room who was holding Katerina in his hands and gently stroking her between her ears. Katerina looked content and Irene saw no fear in her eyes. Another door opened and Irene saw a third alien joining them. The third one had a cat in his hands. It looked almost like Katerina, just a little bit bigger. Irene stretched her hands toward Katerina and the alien gently placed her in Irene's arms.

"She cannot respond to you with her voice yet, Irene. She just an hour ago had a little change in her vocal cords. She will be fine in a few hours. Please trust me. We made sure of that. We don't make mistakes of that nature. You'll see it in the morning," said Forra.

"In the morning? Are we going or should I say are we flying home now?" asked Irene.

"Of course, Irene, you are going home. We never take or as you call it 'abduct' humans for a long time. We value your life more then some of your Earth people do on your planet. We never bring harm to any one. If you did see something like that in your movies, please don't believe in any of that. We haven't had any wars for nearly fifty thousand Earth years and you are still fighting each other everyday somewhere on this beautiful planet. Unfortunately, we cannot help you to stop your horrible fights. It has to come from within you, Irene. On Tycho we don't know what crimes are. You on your planet have jails filled with your criminals. We have no orphans on our planet and your planet is full of them. There is no suffering on Tycho and your planet is filled with pain."

"My Grandmother Rose told me that we have plenty of problems in this world. She said when she'll die she will go to heaven where there would be no pain, suffering, or wars. When I hear you talk about Tycho, it sounds like the place my grandmother wants to go to. The difference is that she has to die to get to a place like yours and you can just live 700 healthy years and enjoy your heaven. I don't think it is fair," said Irene.

"My dear Irene. Many years ago our planet also had the same problems like your planet Earth, but we had very good, charismatic leaders and they led our planet out of the horrible darkness to the light of peace and prosperity. Just think for a moment, if all those enormous resources which your government, and governments of many other countries, spends on weapons were spent on research, or building and growing your food supplies," said Forra.

"I hear those things many times from my father and mother. They talk about it almost every week. It would be great if politicians in every country had chosen rulers like my parents," lamented Irene.

The third alien, who had been silent up to this point, spoke. "It is a very interesting observation, Irene. Unfortunately for you, politicians are chosen not on the basis of their merits. For the most part it is an inherited power. They continue to fight and spend money on destructive and very expensive weapons. Yes, you do benefit from some of the discoveries that are made in the field of the development of military weapons, but it is still so meager compared to what those resources could do for your countries if they would be spent wisely, Irene. It is a tremendous waste of your resources. It is just very unfortunate that people on your planet are so divided culturally and in many other aspects of life in general. We understand that you have a lot of good on your planet but also a lot of dark and very destructive forces. You must learn how to bring all people together and together join your efforts in the name of peace and prosperity for your planet. You have no choice but to overcome the dark forces or you will destroy your planet," said the alien and Irene thought that he sounded like a prophet. She looked at him, not sure if she should ask another question. The alien responded as if he again read Irene's thoughts.

"I'm not a prophet, Irene. I'm just an intelligent mind from the future as you see it." He looked at Irene and read another question.

"Now, Irene, it is going to be our last answer to your last question and we have to depart. Do you want to ask me or you trust me that I can read your thoughts?" asked the alien.

"Do you come from very far away?" asked Irene.

"Yes, we do come from very far away. You cannot see us from where you are but we can see and observe you all the time, Irene. You don't have the right technology yet to see us or any other planets in the galaxies which have intelligent life forms. Your best telescopes are still very primitive. It is not that I'm trying to insult you and your civilization, it is a just an honest observation. Let me try to explain it to you in a simple way. Your best telescope would look like a pair of theater binoculars to us. How far can you see with your theater binoculars, Irene?" asked the alien.

"Not very far. You cannot even watch the birds very well with those binoculars anymore." Irene paused and looked at Forra. "You called us your ambassadors. Are we really your ambassadors and what can we do, or what do you want us to do?"

Forra smiled and replied. "Yes, Irene. You and your Siberian cat Katerina are special ambassadors of our good will. We are sending you back home and including a unique greeting card from all of us with a very extensive message for your people."

"Greeting card?" Irene was surprised that the alien even knew about greeting cards.

"Yes, Irene. Our greeting card is your Siberian cat Katerina. We would like your people to see and to think of what we could do with your cat," replied Forra.

"Yes, I understand. If this is what you could do with my cat, just think what can you do for all the people on our planet? Did we really visit Brazil, Iceland and Russia or was it just a dream?" asked Irene looking at her angel. Forra touched her hand and smiled.

"It is for you to decide, Irene."

"We tried our best to make your stay here a very pleasant one. Have you recently been on an exciting trip, Irene?" asked the second alien.

"In more then one way and I don't know what to believe or think anymore. If it was a dream, then I have to say it was the most incredible dream I've ever had. It is very hard for me to accept that it didn't happen to me at all." She looked at her new friends from another world and blurted out, "Please tell me, do we have real angels among us?"

The aliens looked at each other, their eyes sparkled and they shrugged their shoulders. "Your answer you'll find in time. You'll be fine, Irene. Your cat, Katerina, will be fine, too. Now you have a very different cat Katerina in a very good way. She is what you are going to have as cats 9000 years from now, that is if you don't obliterate yourself into ashes. Human beings, too, will evolve and be very different by then, having developed their minds to their full capacity. I know it is too much for you to absorb at this time, Irene. After all, you are just a child. But we have hope and this is why children's minds, dreams and efforts could make such a big difference in your world. You, Irene, and other children like you are the good force of the future. If I were in your place, I would be thinking the same way and it would be extremely hard for me to accept everything I would have heard on this spaceship. And now, my dear friends, our time has run out. Please, I'd like both of you to close your eyes and go to sleep. You'll not remember anything you have heard here tomorrow morning but slowly, in due time, you will recall your visit with us. We will meet again." With Forra's last words, Katerina and Irene closed their eyes and immediately went to sleep. They went back to where they were in their dream, still holding to the hands of an angel and flying in the cold air of December.

~ ~ ~

When Irene awakened the next morning, she found herself in her warm bed. She could not remember exactly what happened last night to her and her cat Katerina, but she did remember that she traveled with an angel from the Christmas tree around the world. She tried to see her cat Katerina but she wasn't on her bed or anywhere in the room. She looked around her room and didn't notice anything different but felt that something extraordinary happened last night. All she could remember was that it was most wonderful and exciting. She thought of the magic dream she just had and didn't want that dream to come to an end. She closed her eyes and wanted to continue her dream and the exciting journey but she saw nothing in front of her closed eyes. It looked like the show was over and the curtain had to come down. She didn't think that anyone would believe her anyway. After all, she traveled around an entire planet in just a fraction of time. She closed her eyes. A vision of a beautiful angel appeared in front of Irene's eyes and she saw her smiling and waving to her as if the angel was inviting her to open her eyes, get out of the bed and start her new and very exciting day. She opened her eyes again and saw the sun brilliantly shining through the window as if it, too, was trying to tell her that it was time to get out of bed, for another day was about to begin and she should rush forward to greet it.

~ ~ ~

Irene jumped out of her bed and, still in her nightgown, ran down the steps to her Christmas tree calling on her way to her Siberian cat Katerina. She found her sleeping under the tree, tucked into the shape of a bagel. She slowly walked to her and heard her musical purring. She, like Irene, didn't want to wake up on this morning and part with her sweet, cat dreams.

Irene moved closer and gently placed her hand on Katerina's soft, furry body.

"Good morning, sleepy cat," she whispered.

Very slowly Katerina opened one eye, straightened her body and replied. "Good morning Irene, my sweet little sister."

Irene suddenly recognized the voice from her dream but now it was not in a dream. She looked at Katerina and stood speechless, not able to believe what she was hearing with her ears. Katerina closed her eye and went back to sleep. Irene knew that Katerina probably didn't want to part from her adventurous dream.

"Good morning, Katerina. We have a lot of things to do today. It is time to get up and start our day," said Irene loudly.

"Good morning, good morning, Irene. Is it time to get up already?" asked Katerina, her eyes still closed. "I don't know what happened to me last night but my throat is a little bit sore. What do you think it is, Irene? Is it possible that I'm coming down with my first winter cold?" asked Katerina very softly.

"I don't know, Katerina. I don't think cats get colds like people do, but it worries me. Let me warm up some milk for you. I hope warm milk will make you feel better. If you'd like, you can sleep longer. My grandmother Rose always told me, 'If you don't feel well, Irene, take medicine and go to sleep. In your sleep you'll get well.' She thinks that in our sleep our body cells rejuvenate and we become stronger and healthier," said Irene and gently stroked Katerina's fur.

"Well, I guess all good dreams must come to an end," said Katerina and opened her eyes.

After hearing Katerina a few times Irene was convinced that her dream had not been just an ordinary dream, but a dream which only a few very chosen and fortunate individuals experience during their lives. She suddenly felt her heart beat and knew that she definitely was one of them. She took Katerina in her hands and started dancing around the Chrismas tree singing. "Katerina, Katerina, you can talk, you can talk!"

"Oh, Oh. Please don't move that fast, Irene. You are making me feel very dizzy. Sorry my dear, Irene, but I'm just not well today. I feel so different from what I was yesterday. I wonder what could that be? What do you think, Irene?"

Irene stopped dancing and glanced at the top of the Christmas tree. The angel was still on top of the tree but this time she didn't move or smile, she just stood as a beautiful Christmas decoration. Irene looked at her sweet little cat Katerina in her arms and still had a hard time believing that the angel, Katerina and she had just traveled so far and to so many different and exciting places.

"Was it just a dream, Katerina?" asked Irene. Irene's parents entered the room, having heard the commotion and coming to see what was going on.

"Good morning, Mom and Dad. We have a surprise for you. I'm Irene's new sister," greeted Katerina.

At first, Irene's parents thought it was Irene's clever joke and that she learned a ventriloquist's trick from somewhere and had already mastered the art of how to talk without moving her lips.

"I'm glad we have another daughter, Irene," responded Maria.

"It is not Irene. It is me talking, Katerina and I'm real," said Katerina, this time in a stronger tone of her beautiful voice. Maria and Peter both heard the new voice again and looked very confused. They looked at Katerina this time and she continued.

"Thanks to Irene, I can be like her and you. Now I can talk with all of you about a lot of interesting things."

For a few moments Irene's parents stood totally silent and really dumbfounded, not knowing what to believe. They looked at each other and Katerina read their thoughts.

"Mom and Dad. No. No. Both of you don't have to see the doctor and have your heads examined. You are absolutely well this morning. I can assure you of that. I'm the reason for your confusion. From now on, you just would have to get used to the fact that you have another daughter in your house." Katerina paused and waited for their response, but Peter and Maria stood speechless. She waited politely a few more seconds and continued as if nothing extraordinary happened at all.

"By the way, first things first. My throat hurts and I have to go to the bathroom and I need to brush my teeth. It is so much to do for the first time in my life. Is there a tooth brush for me somewhere here in the house?" asked Katerina and looked at Maria. Maria nodded yes and silently went upstairs to get the toothbrush for Katerina. "And I have one more important item to discuss. Please, no more litter box for me. I'd like privacy just like everyone else."

"It's okay, Katerina. We understand," said Irene. "And I can help you brush your teeth since you have no thumbs and will need someone to place the brush between the toes of your paw and to squeeze the toothpaste out. Ooh, it's going to be such fun to have a little sister!"

"And please, don't you worry, I'm not going to fall down the toilet and be drowned. I saw many times how Irene went to the bathroom. One doesn't need a college education to master it, right?" asked Katerina.

"Right, Katerina. I don't have a college degree and you wouldn't have to have one to go to the bathroom by yourself," said Irene, nodding yes and letting Katerina know that she was in total agreement with her.

"I'm not going to miss and pee-pee on the toilet seat either. I promise. I even know how to flush the toilet," giggled Katerina. With those words she looked at Irene again, asking her with her eyes to let her down on the floor. Irene very gently let her down on the floor and Katerina slowly waked toward the bathroom on the first floor. Irene and Peter stood silently trying to hear what was going on in the bathroom. In a few minutes they heard the toilet being flushed and the sound of running water.

Irene's father, Peter, had been standing frozen during this conversation. Finally, he rubbed his eyes as if he was trying to wake up. "My god. What is happening here in our house? Did the Barnum & Bailey circus come here to Goochland County?" exclaimed Peter. "Should we start selling tickets to the most incredible 'Siberian Cat Katerina Show'? Please tell me if I'm going mad or that the most incredible, miraculous thing has happened under our roof!" Peter was pulling his hair and walking in circles. He shook his head in total disbelief as to what he just heard from cat Katerina. Maria came downstairs with the toothbrush in her hand and wordlessly handed it to Irene. An expression of shock still could be read on Maria's face.

Peter continued pacing. "I have only seen things like this in cartoons and on the funniest home videos. One time I saw a cat that was screaming before taking a bath "no, no" and it sounded so real I was in total shock to hear it. But this is not just 'No, no.' She is speaking like a human." Peter stopped and grabbed his wife by her shoulders. "What am I saying, Maria? In my wildest dreams I could never see something like this happening to us." He put his finger to his lips asking for silence and they heard the sound of the water running from the bathroom faucet.

"She didn't even forget to wash her…." Peter looked at Irene not knowing how to respond and Irene came to his rescue.

"Yes, Dad, she didn't forget to wash her paws."

"Or maybe she is brushing her teeth?" added Peter. "Do cats use toilet paper?"

"I guess you would have to ask Katerina about that when she comes here." With that, they heard Katerina's soft tip top and saw her smiling and looking at them.

"I could read your minds from the bathroom. I know exactly what you were talking about. Trust me, I saw how it was done before by Irene and I'm not going to tell you all my little secrets," she said playfully and flicked her furry tail. "One thing for sure I would like to stay away from is cooking and the hot stove. I'm afraid to have my furry coat catch on fire." Everyone nodded in agreement that that would be a terrible thing.

"Now, I feel very hungry. What are we having for breakfast this morning?" were the next words to come from Katerina's little mouth.

"What would you like to have? Is your throat still sore?" asked Irene.

"Thank you for asking, Irene. It feels a little bit better now. I'd like to have something soft and something warm to drink. I don't want to scratch my throat."

"Why would your throat hurt Katerina? Should we call the vet or should we make an appointment to see our doctor?" asked Maria.

"I don't know why it hurt but I'm feeling better by the hour. It is already much better then when I first woke up in the morning. I think we should wait it out today and if I'm not better by tomorrow morning then you can call the doctor," said Katerina.

"Well, I guess we can wait until tomorrow, Katerina. For breakfast, Irene is going to have a bowl of cereal and Peter and I are going to have Peter's wonderful home made lox and bagels," answered Maria. "I think I decided to marry your father the first time I had his lox. It is absolutely delicious. He uses Grandma Rose's recipe."

"I'm sure it's wonderful," purred Katerina, "and for me you can skip the bagels."

"Absolutely, Katerina. Anything that your sweet little heart desires. I'm at your service, it will be my pleasure to make it for you," replied Maria.

"Can I help you make breakfast?" asked Irene.

"Sure, you are the older sister now, I wouldn't mind you helping me to take care of Katerina," said Maria and saw Irene's happy face.

"Well, girls, you can work on the breakfast but I need to collect my thoughts. I'm going to my little studio and practice my violin. When I play violin, I use the time to reflect on what has happened and what I have to do next. In fact, I am going to have to rethink my entire relationship with you girls," said Peter.

"Can I go and listen to you play before our breakfast?" asked Katerina.

"If you'd like, Katerina. I'm so used to seeing you in my little studio when I practice. Now, you can count all my wrong notes and report them to our conductor," Peter joked.

"I love to hear you play. I saw how recently you watched the movie *Young Frankenstien* and wrote the music from the theme for your violin on music composition paper. I just love that melody, it is sooooooo beautifuuuuuul," said Katerina softly.

Katerina followed Peter into his small studio where he kept his violin and his music library. He opened the door and Katerina gracefully jumped on her favorite puffy chair. She got comfortable in her chair and was waiting for Peter to open his violin case. His mind was wandering in many different directions as he slowly opened the case and got out his violin bow. He reached for the rosin and started putting it on the bow.

"Why do you put rosin on your bow?" asked Katerina.

"We have to put rosin on the horse hair on our bow to have more friction between our bow and the strings. If we never put any rosin on our bow we would not be able to get any sound from the violin. It would sound like a very weak whistle coming from very far away," Peter explained.

"Oh, now I understand. I often watched you do it before but could never ask you why you put rosin on your bow. Now I have my answer. Thank you."

"Now you can ask me questions about music and just anything else you want to know. Just please ask me, Katerina. Hopefully, I would have the right answers for all of your questions and if not, I'll do all I can to find the right answer." He took the shoulder rest from the violin case and started to put it on his violin.

"And what does that do for you?" asked Katerina pointing to the violin shoulder rest.

"Shoulder rest was a very important invention, Katerina. It helps violinists hold the violin firmly under the chin. As you can see, I have a long neck and it is very uncomfortable for me to play the violin if I don't have any support between my violin and my shoulder."

"Another question. What kind of strings do you use on your violin?"

"Once again, Katerina, a very interesting question. Nowadays there are a few manufacturers of violin strings. Some of them make metal strings, some nylon and some make both. The violinist decides what strings he or she prefers to use. I used to play on metal, now I use nylon. Metal strings have longer life and break less often." Peter plucked his thinnest string on the violin and continued. "This is an E string. It is the thinnest string on the violin and breaks more then any others. It is a nightmare for the concert violinist or soloist when it breaks in the middle of the concert."

"Really? What does the violinist do when that happens?" asked Katerina.

"Sometimes the concertmaster of the orchestra gives the soloist his own violin, sometimes they have to stop the concert, put on a new string and continue the concert. What else can you do, Katerina?" asked Peter.

"I guess there's nothing you can do about it but just what you said, trade instruments with an orchestra violinist and continue."

"Yes, continue, but what if the violin is very bad in comparison to the one that the solo violinist was playing? What would you do then, Katerina?"

"Then it is bad luck for the violinist and he or she should stop, put on a new string and continue on the repaired instrument."

"I would agree with you on that, Katerina. But no matter what, it is like a disaster striking in the middle of the concert."

"Did you see it happen many times on the concert stage?"

"No, Katerina. I saw it once or twice in my entire life. It mostly happens when you practice and it therefore is wise on occasion to put on a fresh set of strings and don't wait until they die on you when you want them to stay alive and play for you. Have you learned a lot this morning?" Katerina nodded yes and decided to continue her conversation a little longer.

"If you only knew, Papa Peter, how much I would love to play the violin. It so unfortunate to be born as a cat and not have any fingers. My paws are too wide and too short for playing the violin. And, of course, I don't have any thumbs, either." Katerina looked at her paws sadly.

"That is okay, Katerina. You still can do many other great things. All you have to do is just think what is it you really love and want to do and put your mind into it. You see, Katerina, my mother Rose wanted me to be a doctor. When I saw how hard she had to work as a doctor in Russia and how little she got paid, I decided that playing the violin was going to be the best thing for me. And, you know how much I love playing my violin, but unfortunately for me, I should have listened to my mother and became a doctor and I could still play my violin. Doctors in America make good money and I know many doctors who are very good doctors and also are good musicians. And that is not all. They can afford to buy beautiful instruments. One of my doctor's friends had one of the most expensive Italian violins ever made, by the legendary maker Guarneri Del Gesu. The most famous violinist of all times, Nicolo Paganini, owned one of his violins. Now there is a very well known international violin competition named after Nicolo Paganini and it is held in the city of Genoa where Paganini was born. The winner of the competition gets to play Paganini's violin. His violin is priceless." Peter finished his frustrating speech and was ready to start playing. He thought for a second which music to play for Katerina and started to play her favorite. A beautiful melody filled the room. Katerina felt so uplifted that she started to sing the melody with Peter's violin as a duet. She started to sing very softly, trying not to strain her voice. Peter was playing his violin very soft, making sure that Katerina's voice could flow above the sound of his violin.

"Ta, re-ra-reee-ta-re-ra-reee, ta re-ra-reee-ta-reeee, ta-re-ra-reee-ra, re-ra-raaa-ta-re-ra-reee-ta-raaa." Her very unique and beautiful voice was getting stronger and stronger, filling the room. Peter closed his eyes and continued to play, moving the melody a half step up. Katerina saw his eyes were closed and joined him by closing her eyes and totally melting into the beauty of the music they were making together. When they both ended playing and singing and opened their eyes, they saw Irene and her mother Maria standing in the doorway, with tears running down both of their faces.

"It was so beautiful, Papa," said Irene.

"Yes, Irene, Papa plays this melody so passionately and beautifully, like it was written for him," said Katerina.

"The two of you should play it at the concert together," suggested Maria.

Peter smiled and put his violin back in the violin case. "It may be sooner then you think, Maria. A voice like Katerina's is born once in a hundred years. It sounds like it came from heaven or some other world. I just can't believe that of all places it was born here in Goochland County in Virginia. I may have to quit the Symphony just to accompany Katerina. Are you going to give me half of your concert fee to pay for the farm like Irene does?" asked Peter and winked at Katerina, who nodded yes.

"Well, my poor violinist and famous cat Katerina, please follow me. I don't want you two to die here from starvation. You are about to be served the royal breakfast," said Maria and gestured for them to follow her into the kitchen. In the kitchen, Peter saw that there was another chair at the table, one that Irene had used when she was a baby. Now it was going to be Katerina's chair. Katerina jumped up onto the seat of the high chair. The four of them now sat comfortably around the table. Katerina saw that her lox was already cut for her into a few small pieces. She tasted it and rolled her eyes, letting Maria know how good it was.

"I wish this song you just played together had words," said Maria.

Peter shook his head no. "It is great as it is. There are a lot of great melodies that don't have any words and people hum the melodies. What do you think, Katerina?"

"That piece had always been my favorite so it didn't matter to me whether there were words or not." answered Katerina between bites of lox.

"Would you like to come to one of the orchestra rehearsals or perhaps a concert with me and Irene?" asked Peter and Katerina saw that his mind was in deep thought, thinking about her future.

"Yes, I would. I would indeed. But would they let a cat come to the concert hall? After all I don't look exactly like your average concert goer."

"Please leave that to me, Katerina. I'm sure we can arrange it. After all, you are not just a cat. You are the star that can steal the entire show. I'm sure more people would buy tickets to see and hear you sing then to hear just us poor musicians of the symphony orchestra. When Christmas vacation is over and we start playing again maybe I will take you with me to my first rehearsal or maybe to the concert. Let me think about it."

"I'm sorry, Katerina, you could not come with me to see the *Nutcracker* Ballet," said Irene. "It is such a great story about a little girl named Clara and her special gift of the Nutcracker soldier that becomes alive on the night of Christmas. It is just like our story."

"Yes," said Katerina, "and soon our story will also be known throughout the world. I don't think there's any way you can keep a singing and talking cat secret." Katerina finished her lox and looked out the window at two birds sitting on the branch of the tree. She turned her head to Irene. "Irene. Can you hear the birds?"

"Yes, I can hear them, Katerina."

"Can you understand what are they saying?"

"No, why would I? I'm not a bird, Katerina."

"Yes, I know Irene. But I can understand what they are talking about." The rest of her family exchanged puzzled looks. "They are talking about how hard this winter has been on them and how much they missed warmth and they are anxiously waiting for spring to come to Virginia."

Peter, Maria and Irene again exchanged glances with each other and didn't say a word. They knew that there were going to be many surprises in store for them. Katerina was not just a simple Siberian Cat. She was the cat touched by an angel.

~ ~ ~

It was still Christmas vacation and Irene did not have to go to school. She spent a lot of time playing with Katerina and watching her devour books one after another. Her lovable, huggable sister cat Katerina was full of surprises. She discovered that it took her two to three seconds to read the page and she spent more time on turning the page then reading it. Books of about 400 pages were read in twenty minutes. After she read the book, she remembered everything she had read. It was almost as if she was some one like the main character from the movie *Rain Man*. Her father explained to Irene that Katerina had a rare ability to remember things once she saw and read them on the paper. He called it photographic memory. Not many people had that kind of gift and for the cat to have that special gift was just extremely hard to explain. But one doesn't have to explain everything. People are still learning about the stars and other planets in the galaxies, for example. Katerina was one of the things that people had to learn and accept as she was. Other then that, Irene and Katerina spent their week like normal kids would, playing a lot of hide-and-seek. Katerina loved to play that game because she was very small and could hide very well.

Sometimes it took a very long time for all of them, Irene, Peter and Maria, to find her. In the beginning, Peter and Maria loved to play the game of Scrabble with Katerina. When they played it, Irene was always sitting next to Katerina. They laughed a lot and whispered to each other their secrets about their strategies on winning the game. Irene helped Katerina to move the little square letters on the board. That was her largest contribution to their team. It was fascinating for Irene to see how letters would become words. After a few days of gulping books, Katerina's vocabulary grew so large that she began winning the game of Scrabble all the time. Irene's father couldn't stand losing the game, so they had to stop playing that game and began playing a new game, Game of the Battleships. Once again, Katerina mastered the game and won almost every game. It looked like luck was always with her or was it an angel helping her all the time? She saw the battlefield and remembered every move she and her enemy played. Nothing could hide from her eyes. Peter even said once that he thought that Katerina had x-ray vision and could see through things.

Soon the Christmas break was over and Irene had to go back to school. Katerina began feeling lonely. She had read all the books that she could put her paws on in the house and started to look through Peter's music library. She found on his shelves a few orchestra scores and memorized them as easily as any book she has read.

Then she discovered the videotapes recorded by Peter over the years. She started to watch a tape and accidentally clicked on the fast forward button. The content of the tape ran in front of her eyes with the speed of a rocket but Katerina continued to watch it absorbing what was on the tape. Her mind was in total control of properly processing all that she was seeing on the TV screen. Katerina was so involved in the movie that she didn't notice as Irene walked into the room. For a second, Irene couldn't understand why Katerina was fast forwarding the videotape and still sitting in front of the TV screen. Something didn't look right.

"What are you doing, Katerina?" she asked.

"Oh, hi, Irene. I'm so glad to see you back from school. I'm going out of my mind sitting here by myself. Papa Peter at his rehearsals, Mom teaching school. You are being educated in school and I'm here alone. Please join me in watching this movie."

"Are you sure you are watching the movie and not forwarding the tape, Katerina?"

"No, I'm just watching the movie, Irene. First I tried to see it at normal speed and discovered that I had to sit and watch it all day. Then when I forwarded it at high speed I found that it looked the same for me. I can watch it at any speed. Is it something different from how you would watch it?"

Irene nodded yes, not knowing how to explain what she just had seen. She sat down next to Katerina and realized that Katerina could adjust her eyes and brain to any speed. It was another absolutely amazing discovery of the day. She didn't know if she should mention it to her father or not. "How many movies have you seen since I have been at school today?"

"You mean tapes?"

"No, movies. There are two or three movies on each tape."

"Well, I watched twenty tapes so that's more than 40 movies. It didn't take me that long. One of them was a movie about Count Dracula and it scared me." Katerina shivered.

"I don't watch movies like that, Katerina. They scare me, too. Maybe next time you should be more careful what you watch," she said and petted her cat.

"I was just going through the tapes one by one and didn't think of it. It didn't have any title, Papa Peter must have recorded it on the tape," said Katerina.

"I know, sometimes Papa likes to watch these gory movies. He laughs at them and thinks how stupid it is to spend so much money on making that kind of, as he calls it, junk."

"If you call it junk then I have been to a junk yard today." Katerina laughed.

"I'm sure you were, Katerina. Are you going to be scared to sleep alone tonight?" asked Irene and Katerina nodded yes.

"Would you let me sleep with you, Irene?" asked Katerina.

"Yes, we can cuddle through the night and not see gory horror stories but instead have nice sweet dreams together."

~ ~ ~

It was one of those special Saturdays when Peter had to play a concert in the Symphony Orchestra, or as he sometimes called his playing in the symphony orchestra, using a line from an old TV commercial, it was his *Time to make-a donuts.* He came home after rehearsal for lunch. While they were eating their lunch, Peter asked, "Who wants to come to the concert this evening?"

"I would love to come to the concert this evening," said Katerina excitedly.

"Can we take Katerina into the concert hall, Dad?" asked Irene.

"Yes, we can. I had to ask special permission from the Richmond Symphony office to take Katerina to the concert and they said yes. Everyone wants to see Katerina. News traveled very fast about our wonderful Siberian cat Katerina."

"Do we have to have a dress for Katerina?" asked Irene.

"To me she looks great as she is. I think Katerina can be held in the arms of Irene. She doesn't need to be wearing a fancy dress and sitting by herself," replied Peter.

"What are you playing this evening?" asked Maria.

"A very good concert program. One of them is a very interesting piece of music written by the very famous French composer Hector Berlioz. It is called Symphonie Fantastique. I think you all will just love it. It has everything. It is beautiful, romantic and some parts of it very scary. It is written for a very big orchestra and I'm sure that music will reach your hearts."

"I can't wait to go to the concert," said Katerina.

"We all will have a lot of fun and it is about time we introduced Katerina to Richmond society. Right, Katerina?" said Peter.

"If you say so, Papa Peter. Where can I learn more about Symphonie Fantastique. Do you have any book I can read before we go to the concert?" asked Katerina.

"You mean do I have a book on Berlioz you can gulp? No, but you can go on the Internet, enter in one of the search engines Symphonie Fantastique and I'm sure you'll find it there."

"Internet?"

"Sure, the Internet. Ask Irene to show you how to get on the Internet."

"Would you, Irene?"

"Yes, if you promise me that you will not live in cyberspace and forget me."

"I promise Irene. I will only go on the Internet when there is no one in the house."

"Then it is a deal. After lunch, we go on the Internet and explore it."

That evening for the first time she saw Papa Peter in his special evening clothes called tails and it looked so different from anything she had seen before. Papa Peter looked very handsome.

Part 2

Visit to the Orchestra Hall

It was the month of January in Virginia but the weather that day was unusually warm. It was not that the cold days were over, it just simply looked like Mother Nature decided to play a joke and confuse the trees and birds. On TV they announced that the temperature was at the record high of 81degrees. It really felt like summer, but Peter's orchestra schedule calendar on the refrigerator was telling everyone in the house that it indeed still was winter.

"God, I can't believe this weather. It is warm enough to go to King's Dominion," said Peter.

"What is King's Dominion?" asked Katerina.

"It is a great amusement park not very far from us," answered Irene.

"Hm, what can be so amusing in an amusement park?" asked Katerina again.

"It has a lot of different rides. Some of them are rather scary and I'm afraid to ride them."

"Would you be afraid to go on those rides if I would come with you to the park?" asked Katerina.

"Yes, I still will be afraid. I'm not even tall enough to enter some of those rides. You have to be tall and reach their measuring stick or they will tell you that you are too small to go on the ride," said Irene.

Katerina thought for a moment and sadly added, "I don't think I can grow to be that tall that they will let me go on those rides."

"It is okay, Katerina. You can watch me go. And, there are some kiddy rides where we can ride together, right, Dad?" she asked her father and he nodded yes.

"Do you have your music?" asked Maria. Peter looked in his violin case and showed her his music.

"See, Katerina, once before he forgot his music and blamed it on me. Now I always check if he has it with him before he goes to play his concert," said Maria.

"Okay, girls, are we ready to go?" asked Peter.

"Yes, yes, we are," replied Katerina happily. It was the very first time she was going to be out of their house. She knew that Peter and Maria were very protective of her growing fame because it also had a lot to do with their daughter, Irene.

They did last minute checking and all stepped out of the house. At 6:30 in the evening it still felt very warm. Peter opened the back door of his car, a Saturn station wagon, and Irene got in. Katerina jumped into her lap.

"Seat belts, please," said Peter looking through the rearview mirror and making sure that Irene and Katerina were putting on their seat belts. Katerina could not use a regular seatbelt so Peter had bought for her a special harness made just for small animals. Maria got in the front passenger seat and Peter drove out of their farm toward the highway. The concert hall was all the way in downtown Richmond. Soon they were on the highway and for the first time in her life, Katerina saw many cars passing by them. Because of the high speed the drive to the concert hall seemed to be short. They approached the concert hall parking lot and Peter gave to the parking lot attendant his parking pass and drove to the basement where most of the musicians usually parked. He got out first and opened the door for Maria and Irene. They got out of the car and went to the nearest elevator. Irene was holding tight to Katerina, whispering in her ear something that Peter and Maria couldn't hear. Phillip, the first oboe player and one of the oldest friends of Peter, was in the elevator holding the open button and waiting for them to walk in.

"Here you are, Peter. Are you bringing to the concert your new find, Siberian Cat Katerina?" asked Phillip. Peter winked and pointed to Katerina, who was resting in Irene's arms.

"Is it true that your cat can speak and sing?" continued Phillip. Peter smiled and looked at Irene. She turned her head to Katerina and whispered softly to her.

"Yes, I can speak, but I don't sing in elevators," said Katerina. She saw the surprised expression on Phillip's face and continued. "What instrument do you play?"

"A, a…" Phillip stuttered.

Peter interjected, "Phillip is one of the best oboe players I ever heard." He showed them Phillip's small case.

"Hmm. To me it looks very small to carry a musical instrument." Katerina batted at it with her paws.

"Very smart observation, Katerina," replied Phillip and raised his oboe case so that she could see it well.

"It is not like a violin. We can take the oboe apart and put it in the case. This is why it fits in such a small case. Flute players who play piccolo flute are the luckiest ones in the orchestra. Their piccolo case looks just a little bit bigger then a cigar box. Can you imagine being a bass player and carrying this humongous instrument for years? Would it break your back, Peter?"

"It may. You never know. I'm so glad I don't play bass. Bass is like having another person on your back all the time. You have to have big muscles and a big car to carry it and if you are on the airplane, you have to buy for your bass a separate ticket so that it can sit like a king. I always felt very sorry for the bass players." The elevator reached their floor and they all stepped out. More people were coming from other elevators and saw Katerina in Irene's arms. None of them thought that she was going into the concert hall like they were to hear the concert. They took a short walk and Peter led them to the back entrance of the concert hall. He opened the door and Katerina and Irene saw a lot of musicians' eyes focused on them.

"Welcome to the concert, Katerina." Irene heard a familiar voice. She turned around and saw Lynda, another friend of her father's, who played bassoon.

"Wow, what a long instrument," commented Katerina.

"Yes, it is very long, but we can take it apart and it will fit in the case. If we did not take it apart it would be very hard to transport it around."

"It is still not as bad as carrying a bass," said Irene.

"Yes, it is not as bad but it is still very heavy. Are you going to introduce me to your special friend, Irene?" asked Lynda.

"Katerina the Siberian Cat." She introduced her cat Katerina to Lynda.

"Pleased to meet you. It was my dream to come to the concert and visit with the orchestra backstage and meet the musicians," said Katerina.

"Well, here we are," said Lynda. "Please come with me to our dressing room where we put our instruments. There are a lot of people downstairs dying to meet Katerina." They took a walk downstairs and as they reached a big spacious room where Katerina saw a lot of musicians, she suddenly heard applause. "See, Katerina? You already stole the show. You should be conducting this concert. People would go totally bananas in the concert hall."

They walked into the room where Peter usually put his violin and saw two musicians in there. One of them was Anthony, who played French horn. "Hi Anthony, here is my daughter Irene and her friend Katerina."

Anthony looked at Irene and smiled. "Is this your amazing cat Katerina? Am I right?"

"Yes, I'm Katerina," said Katerina and Peter felt if she didn't have her red fluffy fur on her face, it would probably turn red. Once again he came to their rescue. He knew that Irene and Katerina were very shy girls.

"Is it true, Anthony, that the French horn is the longest instrument once you unwind the metal pipe of the horn?" Anthony nodded yes and continued to blow his horn, trying to warm up his lips for the concert.

Peter took out his violin and got it ready for playing. "Okay, girls, time for me to go on the stage and it is your time to go to the concert hall. Let me take you through another door to the concert hall to avoid all this human traffic." Peter led all of his girls upstairs, letting them into the concert hall through a door that was rarely used. When Irene, Katerina and Maria walked into the concert hall they immediately attracted a lot of attention. One of the ushers came to them and looked at Katerina with a big question in her eyes.

"It is okay for me to be here. The Richmond Symphony orchestra management has permitted me to come to the concerts," said Katerina. The usher had been warned ahead of time that there might be a cat in the audience, but she was dumbfounded to hear Katerina speak. They sat in the first few rows of seats since for the most part those seats remain empty as the concerts rarely sold out.

Katerina took the program and read. "*Night on Bald Mountain.*" She looked at Irene and saw as she shrugged her shoulders as if she was trying to let her know 'Don't ask me, ask my father.'

"What kind of music is that? I should educate myself more about music, but there is simply not enough time in a day to play with Irene and learn all the new things I'm interested in. I can forward the video, but unfortunately I never tried to forward the CD disks. Even for me, listening to all the music could be a mission impossible," Katerina thought to herself. A few people from the audience heard her speaking to the usher and reading the concert program and within a short time there was a small crowd around them. People didn't want to leave them. All their attention was on Katerina.

"Papa was right when he said that more people would come to the concert to see Katerina conduct then their music director," whispered Maria into Irene's ear.

The ushers finished seating people in the concert hall. The lights started slowly to dim and Katerina saw on the ceiling of the concert hall little blinking stars.

Maria saw the question in her eyes and smiled. "I know, I know. Whenever I'm in the concert hall it always makes me think who in the world thought about this nuisance and if there are other concert halls with blinking stars on the ceiling."

The concertmaster of the orchestra walked to the center of the stage with his violin and slowly the sound of musical instruments died out. "It is time for the orchestra to tune," whispered Irene in Katerina's ear. Katerina saw as the concertmaster give Phillip, the oboe player they just recently met at the elevator, a signal and Phillip blew a lonely sound into the crowd of musicians on the stage.

"He is giving an A to which all musicians must tune before they start playing all together," said Irene.

After the orchestra was tuned, the concertmaster sat on his chair and looked through his music. Katerina heard applause and saw the conductor walking to the middle of the stage. He raised his hands to the audience letting them know that he appreciated their attention. The audience quieted down and he began to speak.

"We have very special guests with us this evening. We in the orchestra already heard of them but most of you have not. Please give a warm greeting to Irene and her Siberian cat Katerina." He motioned to the seats in the hall where Katerina and her new family were sitting.

The concert hall broke out in friendly clapping and the conductor gestured for them to stand up to acknowledge the appreciation of the people who greeted them. Maria got off her chair, helped Irene get off her chair and turned her head toward the people in the concert hall. The loud applause slowly died and the conductor turned his back to the audience and faced the orchestra. He raised his hands and very soft and fast music began. It reminded Katerina of thousands of mice running in many different directions. She looked at Irene and heard as Maria whispered, "It is a very spooky piece of music. It is a fantasy that paints a picture of weird stuff happening on St. John's Eve, on Bald Mountain near the city of Kiev. This music is composed by the very famous Russian composer, Modest Mussorgsky. You can also see it with Irene in the Walt Disney movie *Fantasia*."

The music totally captivated Katerina. She closed her eyes and felt like she was in Russia on the Bald Mountain. Music came fast and soft and ended on very soft notes. People started to applaud and Irene whispered in Katerina's ear. "We can see *Fantasia* tomorrow. I always skipped that part because I was afraid to watch it. Maybe we can try to see it together?" Katerina nodded an enthusiastic yes to Irene.

The musicians left the stage. The stage manager and his assistants cleared a path through the middle of the stage in order to roll the big concert grand piano onto the stage.

"Wow, Irene. Look at this giant piano," said Katerina. "It's twice as big as yours."

"Yes, it is the biggest piano, nine feet long, which is used mostly in concert halls," explained Maria to both of them.

The musicians came back to the stage and took their places. The pianist came to the stage and gave a bow to the audience. It was another great piece of music by another amazing Russian composer, Sergei Rachmaninoff. In some parts of the music the pianist's fingers ran so fast on the keys of the piano that Katerina had a hard time following them. She looked at her paws and knew that she could never become a pianist.

The first half of the concert was over and it was a time for the orchestra to rest. This rest also was known among musicians as intermission. As they were leaving the stage, Katerina noticed that the violins looked the same but each had a different shade of colors. She looked at Irene and asked. "Irene, I noticed that the violins look slightly different one from another. Why is that?"

"Oh. My dad told me that all violins were made in different times by many violinmakers and this is why they look so different. All violinmakers use the traditional shape and way of making their instruments, it is just when they are finished they would look different. My dad said that there are very few identical violins. Even if some one made an exact copy and it would look exactly alike, it would sound different. It would apply to any string instrument like violin, viola, cello and bass. They all have their own characteristics just like people or pets. What do you think, Katerina?"

"I'm only three month old, Irene, and haven't lived long enough to learn and know all those thing yet. But in time I will."

"Yes. Life is a great school but try not to take wrong turns on the long bumpy road or you can break your neck. This is what my Grandma Rose always says," said Irene and saw her father walking toward them. He was just in a white shirt without his tails.

"Okay, guys. Not to attract too much public attention to Katerina and Irene, we should go out of the hall until the second half of the concert begins." They all followed him and went through the same door they came in. Once they were backstage, Katerina saw that musicians who played big instruments left them on the stage. She glanced at the army of blimpy basses. Not far from them, a battalion of cellos rested their heads on the musicians' chairs. She recognized three bassoons and four French horns resting in their chairs. In one row she saw three shiny instruments.

"What are those?" she asked Peter.

"Those are flutes. One of them, the smallest one, is called piccolo, which means little flute. They play very high notes. Sometimes if I have to sit near the piccolo, I have to have my earplugs in my ears. The notes are so high and strong that my ears start to hurt."

"What are those?" asked Katerina, pointing to a row of black instruments that looked like thick wooden sticks.

"Those are clarinets. We have them in different sizes also. The biggest one is called a bass clarinet and it plays very low notes, and the smallest plays higher notes." He then pointed to the middle size clarinets. "Those are the normal guys," said Peter and saw as Katerina raised her eyebrows.

"Just kidding, just kidding, Katerina. They are all normal, but you can't say the same for musicians. Some of them can be very temperamental. But they cannot behave very badly, only conductors can, because they are the bosses."

"I see." replied Katerina.

"I'm sure you can, Katerina. One day you may appear as a guest conductor in front of this orchestra and I know you would be good."

On the other end of the stage she saw a lot of different and strange looking instruments. One of them was a very tall instrument with two pipes, each a different length.

"Strange looking musical instrument. It looks more like a very strange creature, doesn't it, Katerina? I think it is called chimes. It is going to be used in the second half of the concert in the piece of music that we are going to play. It has a screaming and ugly sound and plays only two notes, G and C. The player would hit the pipe with a hammer and the sound would be flying into the air. The pipes are empty and, as you can see, very tall. If the player is not very tall, he has to stand up on the chair to hit the pipe at the very top. It should imitate the sounds of big bells. This chime is the closest we can come to the bell."

In the middle of the orchestra, Katerina saw another strange looking instrument. It looked like four big pots covered by skin. "What are those? They look like big pots like one would use in the army to cook food for a lot of soldiers. I saw something like that on TV in a movie."

"You are very observant, Katerina. They do look like big cooking pots, but there is no soup inside them. They are also empty inside and have a skin on top of them. Do you see the small handles around those pots?" he said and pointed to them.

"Yes, I see. What do they do?"

"It is a very good question, Katerina. Each pot is tuned differently by tightening the skin on the top of the pot. At the bottom, they have pedals. When the pedals are pressed it changes the sound, making it higher or lower depending on what is asked by the composer of the piece. The next piece of music has one of the most interesting parts written for this instrument. Actually they are called tympani or kettledrums." As Peter said his last words, the vision of an angel appeared in Katerina's head and her words that she could be one of the greatest tympani players surfaced in her head. She looked at her paws and Peter noticed it.

"Would you like to give it a try? I'm sure John wouldn't mind you hitting a couple notes."

Katerina nodded yes and Peter walked to the kettledrums. Irene gently put her on the bench but it was to low for Katerina to reach the drums. Peter saw it and looked around. His eyes stopped on a small case the size of a book.

"I'm sure Jennifer would not mind if we will borrow her piccolo case for a brief moment." He put it on the stool and placed Katerina on top of it. It was perfect for her to stretch her front paws and reach the skin on the top on the tympani. She softly touched the skin and it didn't produce any sound. She hit it slightly harder and the sound came out from the inside of the pot. She took a deep breath and hit it short and fast with both paws, increasing the power of each hit. The beautiful sound of the tympani rose above the instrument into the air, filling the air with sound. Musicians turned their heads and saw Katerina drumming on the kettledrum. She finished her tympani roll and heard loud applause that came from everywhere, the stage, backstage and the concert hall. At this moment, she knew that she was in love with the tympani and she wanted to become a very good tympani player and perhaps, some day, play a concert with the symphony orchestra.

"Well, well, well. What do we have here?" She saw a man standing next to her.

"Hi, John," said Peter, "you don't mind Katerina trying your tympani, do you?"

"With soft paws like hers, I have nothing to worry about." John looked at Katerina. "She looks like the tympani were made for her. She is a natural tympani player. I would be happy to give her a few free lessons; in fact, it would be my pleasure."

"Thank you for your kindness and generosity," replied Katerina and extended her paw to John. He gently took her soft paw for a hand-paw shake.

Another man came and looked at them. "My goodness, who do I see here? My favorite weather man from TV 6, who is also known in a very small circle of his friends as a good clarinet player. Great to see you here, Mike," greeted Peter. "Sometimes Mike helps us when we are short on clarinet players. As you know, anybody can get sick and it is a hard job to find a good replacement on short notice. Mike always comes to our rescue. Right Mike?" Peter gave Mike his hand for a shake hand. "Please meet Katerina and Irene. They are a package deal. I'm just letting you know it in advance in case if you'd like Katerina to help you one day to do a weather report on your TV station." He looked at Mike and smiled.

"Actually, Peter, it would be great. It would boost our ratings. You never know, maybe she would become the first weather cat announcer in America. Tomorrow I'm going to talk about it with my producer. I'm sure he would love to have you as a guest on my show. Please promise me, Ms. Katerina, that I would be the first to have you on TV here in Richmond."

Katerina looked at Irene and smiled. "Only if Irene would hold me in her arms."

"It's a deal. Let's seal it with a…hmm." Mike looked at Katerina

"Paw-shake, or hand-paw shake or paw-hand shake, which one is more acceptable for you?" she laughed.

"I think paw-hand is the best," said Irene.

"Then let it be paw-hand shake from now on," said Mike and handed his hand to Katerina for a paw-hand shake.

James, the stage manager came to them and pointed with his finger on his watch. "Three minutes before we start the second half, Peter," he said, looking at Katerina.

"Oh my god, time flies so fast. Let me take you back to the concert hall," he said, and his flock followed him to the concert hall. They took their seats and saw a lot of people standing around, looking at them.

"This is the price you would have to pay for being a celebrity, Katerina. I have to warn you that it is just a beginning," said Peter. He quickly walked back to take his violin and be ready to play the second half of the concert. Katerina took the concert program and Irene helped her to find the right page. Her eyes moved to the last piece in the program.

"*Symphonie Fantastique.*" She looked at Irene and Irene shrugged her shoulders.

"I've never heard it, Katerina. I'm only eleven years old."

"It is great to be eleven years old, Irene. You have so much time to learn."

"Episode in the Life of an Artist. Hmm, must be an interesting piece of music," read Irene. She saw that it had five parts and thought that it must be a long piece of music. The conductor walked on the stage and Katerina looked at Peter who was sitting in his place, looking at her and Irene. She whispered into Irene's ear and Irene waved her hand to her dad and he waved back to her with his bow.

The conductor raised his hands and the musicians became one with their instruments, ready to begin. He let his hand move and the music started. The opening of the Fantastic Symphony (or *Symphonie Fantastique* as it is known around the world), *Reveries,* was very slow and dreamy. It sounded as if someone was telling the story from his past. It was a very sad story and the storyteller wanted to make sure that he got your full attention. This is why it was so captivating from the very first notes.

Katerina closed her eyes and saw herself and Irene flying with an angel over Russia. It was her flight over the cold country covered with snow and it felt like no one was outside the houses. Thin strings of smoke were coming from the thousands of houses in the countryside and Katerina placed her furry cat body somewhere in the warmest part of the house. She wondered if anyone else in the concert hall saw the same picture as she did when they were listening to the same music. The first movement ended and she opened her eyes and looked at the stage. The orchestra was ready to begin *A Ball,* the second movement. It was going to be a fancy ball filled with the most beautiful and passionate music. She heard the melody of the waltz, which was played beautifully by the section of violins, violas and cellos. It sounded like they all were trying to compete with each other, to show each other who can play it better. Again, she closed her eyes and imagined herself dancing with a beautiful gentleman cat whom looked exactly like her real father, Siberian cat Vassya. They were dancing in the ballroom of a beautiful, old Russian castle. The parquet floors were so shiny that she could see their reflection in the floor. She looked small and very elegant and her dancing partner was strong, furry and very graceful. So they danced to the music until it stopped and the old castle and her cat gentleman disappeared into the air with the last sound of music.

Sadly, Katerina opened her eyes and found herself in the arms of Irene. She looked on the stage and saw the conductor ready to continue to tell Berlioz's musical story. With the sound of music, she closed her eyes and the music brought her into a beautiful countryside in the middle of summer. She heard the sound of an exciting instrument, and saw trees gently stirred by the wind. The music brought calm into her heart and she felt very secure to be in the arms of her sister, Irene. The music evaporated and Katerina almost jumped out of Irene's arms when the fourth movement of Fantastic

Symphony, *March to the Scaffold,* began. It was crazy and scary music and Irene and Katerina were hanging tight to each other through the entire march. They could hardly breathe.

The music ended and they still were clinging to each other. Little did they know, the real trip was still ahead of them. The fifth and last part of the symphony was *Dream of a Witches' Sabbath.* Katerina's hair rose on her pretty body as if she was ready to fight a big ugly dog. Irene was shivering and grabbed her mother's hand. They saw themselves in the crowd at the witches' Sabbath, in the midst of ghastly spirits, sorceresses, and monsters of every kind assembled together. Katerina saw as the musician hit to death the chimes with a hammer. They were screaming in a most scary and ugly sound. She could not believe that she just saw them recently standing peacefully on the stage. Now strange, grotesque noises, groans and bursts of devilish laughter were coming from the stage. She felt as Irene's body was shivering and transferring her shivers over to Katerina's body. When they thought that they couldn't take anymore of this madness, the music stopped. It was the end of the symphony.

The public in the concert hall broke into very loud applause and the conductor asked the musicians to stand up and take a bow. People wouldn't stop applauding and the conductor asked each section of the orchestra to stand up separately so that people could greet them with their thank you applause. Finally, Katerina saw that the conductor didn't come out. The musicians stood up from their seats ready to leave the stage and Peter waved to them to come back to his dressing room through the back stage door. In the dressing room, Katerina still was under the spell of the music.

"How did you like the concert, Katerina?" asked Peter, putting his violin in the violin case. She was speechless and just slowly shook her head. He gave Maria his violin case and said. "Now I think it would be a good idea if I would hide Katerina in my tails. So many people saw her. It may be hard to leave and get to our car. We have a celebrity now. She is becoming like the *Beatles* of the past. From now on, we have to be careful. We don't want Katerina to be kidnapped."

Irene gently handed Katerina to her father and he slid her inside his tails close to his chest. "Now we are ready to go, girls," said Peter, and they began their short journey to the parking lot. They walked rather fast, hoping not to be recognized by the crowd of people. Soon they were next to their car. Peter opened the lift gate of the station wagon and Maria placed his violin inside. He opened the back door for Irene, let her in and leaned deep into the car. "Now you are free, Katerina. Irene is all yours." He opened the door for Maria and in seconds they were driving out of the parking lot. On the highway they felt more relaxed. Peter looked through the rearview mirror and saw Irene holding tightly to Katerina.

"Are you still scared of the great Berlioz and his crazy *Symphonie Fantastique?"* he asked them jokingly and saw as they both at the same time nodded their heads yes. "It is just music, nothing to be scared about. But I have to tell you, some paintings, music and books are rather scary. Good writers, artists and composers can do it to you. Do you know that Berlioz was a very good conductor, great composer and also a writer? Berlioz was an extremely talented individual and great innovator for his time. No one before him used the orchestra like he did When his Symphony was played the first time, I'm sure it scared a lot of people, not just children. But it is very exciting to play it. Sometimes I feel that his madness may take me with him when I'm playing his music."

They drove in silence for a short time and Katerina decided to ask a question. "Why did he have to write such scary music?"

Peter looked again in the rearview mirror and said. "He wrote it because it is music about the life of an artist. It is about his love, losses, suffering and attempt to poison himself. He sees all those crazy visions after he takes the poison. That is what you heard in the last two parts of the symphony. I have to tell you, I always feel as if the stage is shaking from the racket that is going on the stage. All of the brass instruments, tuba, trombones, basses, drums, kettledrums and crazy chimes screaming all at the same time. I don't want to hear this music in my dream in the middle of the night. But, music is music. It is a great symphony and from the time when it was composed in 1829 I'm sure it has been played at least a hundred thousand times all over the world. Maybe one day Katerina will conduct our symphony and many others around the world. No one would let me conduct the orchestra but I think Katerina's concerts would be totally sold out. I'm sure people would pay big bucks to come to see her and listen to her conducting. I would not be surprised if soon our phone will be ringing off the hook with invitations for Katerina. Can you handle it, Irene? After all, where Katerina goes, you would have to go also. Am I right, Katerina?" said Peter.

"I want to be always with Irene, after all I'm her cat," replied Katerina, looking out the car window and seeing how heavy, dark clouds covered the sky and blanketed the stars, which now were nowhere to be found.

"It is still winter and cold is coming back, Irene. This summer-like weather is a short-lived caprice of nature. I hope trees and little frogs will go back to sleep and survive soon the coming bitter cold to Virginia." Peter looked again into the rearview mirror and was amazed how beautiful those two young girls looked together.

"I'd like to ask you a question. What makes a good conductor of the orchestra?" asked Katerina.

Peter thought for a moment. "Katerina, you touched a very sore subject for a musician. First, the conductor should be talented and have respect from musicians. He or she should trust the musicians, show them respect, and not beat them to death rehearsing his or her personal problems. The conductor should not talk too much about the music he or she is rehearsing and should be able express and show what is wanted just by using the hands, eyes, and body language, like a mime. When a good mime tells you a story, you don't have to hear him talk. When a good conductor is on the podium, he or she doesn't have to talk too much to make musicians do what the music is asking them to do. From my orchestra experience, I can tell you that musicians don't like to be treated like children and lectured like students by a conductor. A conductor is walking a very fine line doing that to the musicians and it may backfire."

"How could it backfire on the conductor. Isn't he the number one figure in the orchestra?" asked Katerina.

"Yes, that is true, but who is going to play the music, the conductor? No, musicians play the music. If the conductor doesn't have the magic key to musicians' hearts, and their respect, it will show in their playing. They will not be inspired to give all they could and all they have. Why are you asking all these questions, Katerina? Are you preparing yourself for a conductor's future?" asked Peter.

"No, but I'm interested to know the relationship between the conductor and musicians and what it takes for musicians to respond to a conductor's wishes."

"You are incredibly observant, Katerina. You are thinking not like a few months old Siberian cat but more as a very mature and super intelligent person," said Peter, looking into the rearview mirror. He saw the blinking lights of a police car. "Oh, oh, girls. Was I speeding?" he asked. "I didn't look at the speedometer, I was listening to your conversation with Katerina. I don't think I've ever asked you the kind of questions as she did, so I was learning." Peter found a safe spot to pull off the road and stopped his car. A young and handsome policeman approached his car. It was a state police trooper. On his name badge Peter read 'Adam'. He rolled down his window. "Hello officer, did I do something wrong?"

"Where are you coming from?" asked the officer.

"I'm coming from work," Peter answered.

"Work?" asked the policeman, looking at Peter's tails. "What kind of work?"

"Papa Peter is a violinist with the Richmond Symphony Orchestra and we are coming from the concert," said Katerina.

The officer looked down to see who was talking to him and saw Katerina in the arms of Irene. "I'm just checking to see if there are any impaired drivers driving on this Saturday evening," he said to Irene.

Irene replied, "I didn't say anything, it was Katerina."

The officer looked at Maria and she said. "I didn't say anything, officer."

"Then who did?" he asked again.

"Katerina did, Katerina the Siberian cat was talking to you."

"The cat was talking to me?" asked the officer. He looked again at Peter. "Are you sure you are telling the truth?"

"Positive, officer. Katerina, please save me," said Peter with a smile.

"Yes, officer, I was the one who responded to your question about where we were coming from. I just heard the most amazing music, the *Symphonie Fantastique* by the great French composer Berlioz. Have you ever heard it?"

They watched as the face of the officer lost its color. He was speechless but slowly shook his head no in answer to Katerina's question.

"You should, officer. I highly recommend it for you. It is great music to hear alive for the first time. It truly can take you to a different world." Katerina sighed.

"Yes, officer, she is right. It would take you to another world and make you dizzy and you don't even have to have a glass of wine to feel dizzy," said Peter. "Now that you can see that none of us have been drinking, can we go please?"

Just then, another car pulled in front them. Two men got out of it and walked toward them. One of the men tapped the police officer on his shoulder and showed him his ID. They exchanged silent eye signals as the officer handed him back his ID.

"I have to put my little girls to bed, Officer Adam. Can we go?" Peter asked again.

The officer nodded and went back to his car.

Peter started the car and pressed on the gas, looking into the rearview mirror to make sure that it was safe to get back on the highway. He saw that the car that stopped in front of them was following his car. He shook his head.

"Well, girls, it is our exit and we are almost home without any ticket. This policeman made me feel nervous. One never knows how things can turn out," said Peter and took his exit off the highway. He looked again into the rearview mirror.

"My cat sense tells me that we are being followed. But I'm sure this is for our own protection. Please don't be worried, I don't feel like those men mean us any harm," said Katerina.

"I expected that to happen sooner or later, Katerina. I knew there would be a lot of people who would like to get their hands on you. I guess from now on we are under the protection of the FBI." They got off the secondary road and were driving on the gravel road, going deep into the woods toward their small but very cozy country house. The car stopped and Peter heard the sound of a helicopter in the air high above them.

"Well, my dear ladies. You are the treasure and I think it must be your armed guards," said Peter and shook his head. He got out of the car and opened the doors for Maria and Irene. Then he got his violin and they all walked to the house. The temperature outside was rapidly dropping and they all were very happy to be back home in a warm place.

"Okay, girls, anyone want a snack?" asked Maria.

"I'd like to have an apple," said Irene.

"I would not refuse a small bowl of cereal with milk," Katerina said and looked at Irene.

"Well, sweet hearts. Let me give you a good night kiss and I'm off to my bed. I feel very tired from the surprise stop on the highway and after a concert like that. It was absolutely exhausting to play all this music. Too many notes to play for one evening. Even my fingers feel tired. I'll see you all in the morning and please don't forget to brush your teeth before you go to bed." He gave a kiss to Irene and stuck his cheek out for Katerina. She reached his cheek and touched it with her wet nose.

"Yes, Daddy," Katerina and Irene replied at the same time. After the snack they both went upstairs to the bathroom, brushed their teeth and for a little while sat and chatted on Irene's bed. When it was time to go to sleep, Irene looked at Katerina and whispered, "Please, can you sleep with me? I feel so scared tonight like my father did when he was a little boy and read a lot of Edgar Allen Poe. I think it is the scary music of the concert. I still can hear the sound of the crazy bells ringing in my ears. Brrrr." Katerina purred "yes," crawled under the blanket and they hugged each other. For a moment there was silence.

"Good night, my sweet, furry sister. I hope you'll not bite me on my nose like the cat Vassya bit my father when he was a little boy," said Irene and closed her eyes.

"Good night, my big sister. I promise that I will not bite you like Vassya. After all, I'm a super intelligent cat," replied Katerina.

"You are not just a cat, Katerina. You are Princess Katerina," added Irene. They slowly closed their eyes in the darkness of the bedroom and saw a vision of an angel. "Are you dreaming about the angel and our trip, Katerina?" whispered Irene, half asleep.

From Katerina, there was no answer, just the sound of contented purring.

Tomorrow was another day with the promise of another exciting adventure crossing paths with their young lives.

ABOUT THE AUTHOR

Leonid Prymak was born in the former Soviet Union. A concert violinist by training, he began writing to explore his personal experiences with the paranormal-experiences beyond scientific explanation. According to his family, his ability to dream about the future was inherited from his mother. One of his inexplicable childhood dreams was that he would live in the United States. That dream came true: he now resides in Virginia. When he is not playing violin with the Richmond Symphony, Mr. Prymak can be found writing, tending to his various business ventures or sharing the gift of his playing at his book signings. Otherwise he spends time with his two children, whom he believes also have inherited paranormal abilities.

The children's book, *Adventures of Siberian Cat Katerina,* is his second work. A window into the future, it is intended for children with curious minds and a desire to learn about many different fields that are not usually explored in school.

His first book, *Forbidden Dreams,* received a very warm reception from the readers and is very prominent on **Amazon.com** The novel, *Forbidden Dreams,* draws heavily on Mr. Prymak's paranormal experiences, but also on his life as a symphony musician in Russia and the United States. Although the characters in his love story *Forbidden Dreams* are loosely based on people he has known, the plot and the characters in it are the fruits of Mr. Prymak's fertile imagination-or, if not, they are perhaps a premonition of some events yet to happen.

0-595-22497-0

Made in the USA
San Bernardino, CA
08 September 2018